LORD I'M NOT DEAD YET

DR. DAVID ROBERTS

LORD I'M NOT DEAD YET

VIETNAM, ABORTION, REPENTANCE, A PHYSICIAN'S LIFE

TATE PUBLISHING
AND ENTERPRISES, LLC

Lord, I'm Not Dead Yet
Copyright © 2014 by Dr. David Roberts. All rights reserved.

No part of this publication may be reproduced, stored in a retrieval system or transmitted in any way by any means, electronic, mechanical, photocopy, recording or otherwise without the prior permission of the author except as provided by USA copyright law.

This book is designed to provide accurate and authoritative information with regard to the subject matter covered. This information is given with the understanding that neither the author nor Tate Publishing, LLC is engaged in rendering legal, professional advice. Since the details of your situation are fact dependent, you should additionally seek the services of a competent professional.

The opinions expressed by the author are not necessarily those of Tate Publishing, LLC.

Published by Tate Publishing & Enterprises, LLC
127 E. Trade Center Terrace | Mustang, Oklahoma 73064 USA
1.888.361.9473 | www.tatepublishing.com

Tate Publishing is committed to excellence in the publishing industry. The company reflects the philosophy established by the founders, based on Psalm 68:11,
"The Lord gave the word and great was the company of those who published it."

Book design copyright © 2014 by Tate Publishing, LLC. All rights reserved.
Cover design by Joseph Emnace
Interior design by Manolito Bastasa

Published in the United States of America
ISBN: 978-1-63449-072-6
Biography & Autobiography / Medical
14.10.15

ACKNOWLEDGEMENTS

I want to thank Ron Bailey for pushing me to look once more at those things that are imprinted in my memory, particularly those memories of my time in Vietnam. Special thanks are due to my wife, Cindy, who not only allowed me the time to write this book but, very importantly, encouraged me as I spent many hours on my first effort at writing a book.

CONTENTS

Introduction 9
Bathing a Cat 11
Eight Grades, Two Outhouses 15
The Bull 19
Hog-Killing Weather 23
The Paw Paw Patch 27
Superman 33
Spitball 39
Restriction 43
The Red Circle 47
Present! Arms! 49
A New Vision 53
The Phone Call 59
College 61
Elizabeth Taylor 65
The Interview 69
A Box of Bones 75
Well! 81
One Floor Down 85
The Clinical Years 89
WPAFB and Mac Dill AFB 95
USSF Camp David Widder 101
The Clinic 109
Language Classes 115

Supply Lines	119
Surgery	127
Nurse Midwives	131
Dr. Jones	135
MEDCAPS	143
Reported Dead	149
My War, Fighting the Friendlies	153
Forty Thousand NVA!	155
Stateside and Angels?	159
Residency	163
A Box of Kleenex	169
Thank God I Failed	171
Abortions and Me	177
Life Goes On	183

INTRODUCTION

> I am weak, but Thou art strong
> Jesus, keep me from all wrong.
> I'll be satisfied as long
> As I walk, let me walk close to Thee
>
> Just a closer walk with Thee,
> Grant it, Jesus, is my plea.
> Daily walking close to Thee,
> Let it be, dear Lord, let it be.

These words from the old gospel hymn, "Just a Closer Walk with Thee," author unknown, have run through my mind many, many times. But, with the perspective gained with age, I now realize that it has been my Lord who was continuously walking close to me, even before I ever knew him and even when I was making every effort to stay as far from Him as I could.

I was named after Dr. David Plumlee of Celina, Tennessee. As a boy, I was told that Dr. Plumlee died when he was in his forties, after being married for only one week. He died after contracting influenza as he worked, taking care of patients during the 1918 inluenza pandemic that killed an estimated fifty million people worldwide. I was inspired by stories about Dr. Plumlee when I first thought of becoming a physician. Later, when I was operating on AIDS patients in Columbus, Gerogia and again in Sanyati Baptist Hospital in Zimbabwe, where it was estimated that seventy-five percent of my patients had AIDS, I remembered that I was named after Dr. Plumlee. Like him, I could not concern myself and could not stop operating just because of the risk that an inadvertent needle stick in the operating room could infect me; he didn't stop because of a known risk. Maybe, just as stories about Dr. Plumlee inspired me, someone may find something in this book that will have meaning in their life.

As I began to reflect on moments in the past, I realized that I needed to tell not just about my time in Vietnam but also of memories of how God brought me to where I am today. I also realized that many of my memories are of funny and not-so funny events that resulted from my own stupid actions. My hope is that as you read this you will not only recall the many occasions in your own life when God walked with you and protected you but that you will also remember and share with others those times that bring you a smile.

BATHING A CAT

Two of the world's greatest parents, Luke and Nelle Roberts, met because of the 1937 flood, which flooded Louisville, Kentucky, along with many other cities along the Ohio River. My father was in law school at the time of the flood, joining others who were involved in rescue efforts. He met Nelle Burden and her mother when he carried them to the safety of a boat, removing them from their flooded home.

In 1940, I was born in Louisville, Kentucky, and taken home to Celina, Tennessee, where my father practiced law and farmed. When World War II started, the farm was sold, and my parents moved to an apartment in New Albany, Indiana, across the Ohio River from Louisville, Kentucky, close to a defense plant where my father would be working.

My first memories are from the age of four, while we lived in New Albany, Indiana. At the time that World War II was in full swing, a young David Roberts was given a toy rifle. The song, "What Do They Do in the Infantry?" was popular, and I remember marching around our apartment, with my gun on my shoulder and singing, "What do they do in the infantry, they march, they march, they march." Who could have imagined that from that time on through high school I would dream of becoming an infantry officer? That dream was suddenly ended, and just as quickly, I was given a new vision—a vision that was to motivate me for what was to become my life's work.

Other memories from my preschool years come rushing back. One such memory is of the day that I climbed up on a neighbor's car and decided to look at my self in the rearview mirror mounted on the door. Holding on to the mirror, I leaned over and was able to admire myself—that is, until the mirror fell off and I landed headfirst on the rocks below. I was covered in blood and scared beyond belief not because I was scared from being hurt but because I couldn't think of any good reason for tearing the mirror off that man's car.

As my scalp wound was healing, my birthday finally arrived. The present I was most proud of was a red sand bucket. Now what can a five-year-old boy do with his brand-new sand bucket besides fill it with sand? Well, the first idea that came to mind was that a neighbor's cat would like a bath. Believing that was a good idea. The cat apparently wanted to end the bath a little sooner than we did and kept trying to claw his way out, scratching two servant-minded boys in the process. When the cat was completely soaped up, we emptied the bucket, and, while one of us held the cat, the other took the wagon and bucket to get rinse water. The neighbor's cat apparently did not enjoy the rinse process as much as we had hoped. When we pushed the cat's head under water to rinse its head, the cat objected and began making an awful racket, exceeded in volume only by the lady that owned the cat. The cat took off running, and so did two boys. Unfortunately, we never saw that cat again, and we never knew if a bath made him look better. Also, unfortunately, the cat belonged to the very same people who owned the car, the one with the missing mirror. My parents explained to me that I should, perhaps, stay away from that end of the apartment building. My rear end understood the discussion better than my brain but soon quit hurting, and my scratches healed.

After an armistice ending the war was announced, my parents drove downtown to join in the celebrations. They took me into a bar where everyone was singing the song, "When Johnny Comes Marching Home Again." My parents sat me on the bar where all the surrounding environment and celebrating could be seen. Never having been in a bar, I was fascinated by the tall stools, the spittoons, and the two large jars next to me. One jar had pickled eggs, and the other had pickled pig's feet. At the time, I couldn't really appreciate all the celebrating, and to this day I still wonder, as I did then, why would anyone would eat a pig's foot.

Large artillery is not loaded with oversized rifle cartridges, but instead the projectile is inserted from the rear of the barrel into the chamber of the gun. After the projectile is loaded, a number of cloth bags containing a measured amount of gunpowder are placed in the chamber. During World War II, my father, a lawyer, worked as the director of the specifications department at the "bag plant," where the various gunpowder charges for artillery were packed in cotton bags. When the war ended, the bag plant closed and we moved to Glasgow, Kentucky, where I was enrolled in the first grade.

EIGHT GRADES, TWO OUTHOUSES

My first grade was not very memorable; I was glad when my parents bought a farm and we moved to the country, where a young boy could enjoy a multitude of fascinating and new things. The second grade found me in a one-room school with eight grades, a potbellied stove, two outhouses, and one teacher. At that time the requirement for a teacher was that he or she had to have a high school diploma.

I learned that my teacher was a tough woman, not one to be messed with. One day, our cute, little, sweet, and very young teacher suspended two eighth grade boys because of discipline problems. All of us knew that something might happen the next morning, and somehow we managed to convince our parents to drop us off at school a little early that day. As we stood outside the school, three cars arrived bringing a number of tough-looking men in overalls. The men walked up the steps and stood in front of the door, waiting for the teacher. When she arrived, she walked up the steps, greeted one of the men, and was welcomed by a profane remark. At that moment, she reached up and slapped him in the face so hard that he bounced off the wall. She opened the door and walked inside, leaving the men behind her. After standing on the steps for a few minutes, the men angrily returned to their cars and disappeared. When the teacher rang the bell, we filed in to begin classes; our teacher calmly started the day, with not the slightest suggestion that anything unusual had happened. She never had any more discipline problems after that.

Anyone born after September first had to start school a year later than those born before that date. Since my birthday was in August, I was the youngest in my class. My parents had taught me to read a year or two before I started school, and I could read better than the other second grade students, so my teacher allowed me to take the second and third grade together. That made school more interesting, but, from that time on, I was always younger than my classmates, in some cases, up to two years younger than everyone else in my classes. Later on when I started high school, I realized that being younger than everyone else had its disadvantages. For example, even though I loved football, it was just not going to be possible for me to play against two-hundred-pound tackles and guards, since I was only five feet two inches tall and weighed ninety-two pounds. There were advantages though; it was much easier to concentrate on my studies, since the girls were older than me and not interested in a boy whose voice hadn't yet changed.

Of all the things that were emphasized in my one-room school, the one that I enjoyed most was penmanship. We were taught to use a simple ink pen that we dipped into the inkwell, which was a fixture on each desk. The nicest thing about a one-room school with eight grades was that I could listen as the teacher was teaching students in higher grades. When the fourth grade class was reading about Tom Sawyer dipping Becky Thatcher's braids into the inkwell, I knew that I just had to try that with the blond-haired girl that sat in front of me. I very carefully stuck the end of one of her long plaited pigtails into my inkwell, making certain that she didn't feel me doing it. When the other students saw me do it, even though they thought it was funny, they made sure that they didn't let on and didn't allow themselves to laugh. When recess came, everyone else knew and so did the girl with ink on her pigtail. I wish I could tell my reader that she forgave me, but it didn't happen. She was mad, and, the next day, she was even angrier because her mom had spanked her and cut off her pigtails.

A small general store next door to the school stands out in my memory. The store had the classic potbellied stove, a pickle barrel, and wooden rocking chairs in front of the stove. That store was a gathering place for men, who would sit around the store, tell tales, and spit tobacco juice on the hot stove. I can remember the spittle sizzling as it ran down the side of the stove. At lunchtime, students would go to the store to buy candy bars and soft drinks; my favorites were always a Baby Ruth and an Orange Crush. Just before we moved from that area, I got an Orange Crush out of the soft drink cooler and forgot to pay for it. For the next twelve years, I worried about the fact that I had not paid for that soft drink. In the summer before starting medical school, I drove the trip of over one hundred miles to go pay for that. The owner of the store was really surprised and tried to tell me to forget it. He did accept the payment though, and I felt much better as I drove away.

THE BULL

Our farm outside of Haywood, Kentucky, was a great place for making memories. We moved into an old farmhouse that was originally a log house. A previous owner had added wood siding on the outside and had plastered the walls on the inside. We moved in before the school year started. When we moved in, I had to use the two-hole outhouse while my father was working to add on a bathroom. By the time the new bathroom was completed, it was winter. For years, those in my family told the story of my first trip to the outhouse in the snow, returning to stating most emphatically, "I'm going to go stay with my grandmother, and, when you get a bathroom, you can call me!"

The house had been lived in for several years by a family of tenant farmers who had pulled off baseboards, door facings, and window facings to use for firewood. They finally left because the house was "haunted." The house at one time had gaslights that had been removed and replaced with electric lights when the Tennessee Valley Authority brought electrical service to Barren County. The gas pipes that ran through the attic, were left in place. Late at night, rats became active and ran along the pipes, causing the pipes to bump on the attic floor. The sound that resulted from the resident rats sounded like ghosts walking around in the attic. At least, that was the story my parents told as they tried to convince me that I should go to sleep and that there were no ghosts or monsters in the attic. I'm still not real sure that the house was not haunted.

There was a tenant farmer family living in a small house located on one corner of the farm. They had a boy called A. J., who was my age; the two of us had many opportunities to get in trouble and took advantage of every opportunity. I won't even try to tell more than a few of those stories. Dad had dairy cattle and a bull that had become mean. A. J. and I would often crawl under the fence, tease the bull, and race back to dive under the fence, where we could feel safe. Fortunately, neither of us ever tripped. and the bull always respected the fence. Needless to say, we never told our parents how brave we thought we were.

That same bull was involved in an incident that allowed me to witness an example of real bravery. I was with my father in the loft of the barn tossing down hay to the cattle below us when the bull came in and began to gore a cow that bull had backed up into a corner of the barn. Dad jumped down from the loft to the floor, about ten feet below us, and attacked the bull with a pitchfork. After sticking the bull about three times with that pitchfork, the bull left. Dad climbed back up the ladder and never said a word about the incident. My father instantly became my hero. Even though he is no longer with us, he is still my hero.

Calves on our dairy farm were separated from their mothers a few days after they were born. A few weeks after weaning, the calves were ready to be moved to a pasture some distance away from the cows. A. J. and I wanted to be involved and asked if we could move them. As we got ready to move the calves, I decided that I could tie a rope around the neck of one of the calves and tie the other end around my waist; that way, the calf would have to stay with me, and the others would probably not run off. We headed off for a pasture and had to go down a fairly steep hill. I never expected that the calves would want to run down the hill and had no idea of how fast calves can run. With that calf pulling a six-year-old close behind her, we made it down the hill in record time. I was running much faster than any boy could and must have been taking steps that were, at least, six feet in length. From the perspective of a much older David Roberts, it is now obvious that God surely protected A. J. and me from the bull that we taunted, and He most assuredly kept me on my feet, preventing me from being seriously injured or killed that day when the calves took me for a run down a rocky hill.

Mom worried that I would be a pest and told me many times that I was to come home at mealtime if A. J. and I were playing. One day, his family was about to eat earlier than usual and invited me to join them. I explained that I was going home, but A. J. promised that he would eat fast and come back out. I decide to wait for him, and, while I was waiting, I brought out my slingshot. About the time I was looking for a target, their rooster walked into the yard. Without any real thought, I pull back and fired a rock at the rooster. My aim had never before been that good. The rock hit the rooster in the head, and the rooster hit the ground. I was struck with fear; I knew that I had killed their rooster. After what seemed like a century, but was probably only a few seconds, the rooster began to flop around. I kept trying to come up with some story about the rooster; I knew that I couldn't tell the truth. Then, just as the door opened, the rooster walked away. I cannot explain the relief I felt when that rooster walked away.

Before we moved to the farm, I had been given a puppy for my birthday, one that grew to become a great cattle dog.

At the time of my birthday, I was in the first grade reading about Spot as in the book *See Spot Run*. Even though the dog had no spots, I named her Spot. My little sister could not pronounce "Spot" and would say, "Pot." Soon, the dog was called Potty. One day, Dad had called a veterinarian without telling my mother. As the veterinarian was driving by the house on the way to the barn, my mother stepped out of the kitchen to give our dog some kitchen scraps. She noticed that each time she called out, "Here, Potty", the car would stop and then start up again. That didn't make sense to her, until later when she told Dad about that strange man and how he kept stopping each time she called, "Here, Potty." I still remember how embarrassed she was when she found out that the strange acting man was named Dr. Pott.

HOG-KILLING WEATHER

Unlike most children, I loved to eat greens. To this day, nothing has changed, and I would really like to dig into a big mess of collard greens. In the spring, pokeweed would appear in every fencerow. While the plants were still small, the leaves made great cooked greens (though today most medical authorities recommend against eating pokeweed greens). I would often take my little red wagon and fill it with leaves from new pokeweed plants. Mature pokeweed plants have red berries that my friend A. J. and I mashed to make a dye. We used the dye to paint our faces to make ourselves look like Indian warriors with war paint. When we proudly came home to show off our work, my mother was horrified. What she knew was that the dye would not wash off. At least, school had not yet started, and Mom could keep me at home with my war paint until it was gone.

There was a large peach orchard on that farm. I don't understand why fruit trees will have a bumper crop some years; however, we had an unexpected bumper crop of peaches and cherries. The peach trees were so loaded with fruit that it was necessary to prop up the limbs, which Dad did by nailing boards to each major branch of the trees. When the peaches began to ripen, people came from other farms with their horse and tractor-drawn wagons; each wagon was filled with bushel baskets of peaches, and picking peaches became a social event. Mom peeled and canned quart jars of peaches every day for weeks. When we moved to Indiana, there were more than 250 quart jars of peaches that made the move. We were still eating peach cobblers for, at least, the next ten years.

Between the house and the outhouse, there was a storage building with a large cherry tree that hung over the roof on one side of the building. The same summer that peaches were so abundant, that tree also put on a bumper crop of cherries. A. J. and I spent a lot of time on that roof, eating cherries and seeing how far we could spit the cherry stones.

Clustered around fence lines were trees, and many were host to wild grape vines. The vines were heavy with bunches of small grapes. To reach those, it was necessary to climb the trees; climbing the trees made the harvesting process more fun. The grapes were small and too sour for anyone to enjoy eating them. A. J. told me that we could make wine from those grapes and keep it a secret from our parents. We found an empty crock previously used for making sour kraut. Once again, the little red wagon was put to work hauling grapes to the tobacco barn where we had the big crock. After the grapes were crushed, we sneaked into the kitchen to steal some sugar to add to the grapes. The covered crock bubbled for several weeks before we let our secret out. We were allowed to taste our product before our fathers claimed it. Apparently, our first and only venture into making wine turned out well.

Farms are always plagued with rats. Rats seem to always congregate in and around corncribs. One day, a number of Dad's friends gathered for a "rat killing." Eight-inch wide boards were laid out around the crib and six-inch wide boards were nailed to each side to make the "rat runs." The rat runs were propped up at the places where the rats would be likely to come out of the crib. A. J. and I went inside, began beating on the corn and the walls, and made as much noise as possible. The rats just poured out, running down the newly constructed runs where men met them with clubs. That day, a farm wagon was loaded with several hundred rats, which were then taken to a field to be buried.

The rat killing was followed later that day by a squirrel hunt. None of us, including two older boys related to A. J., had a license or a gun. The older boys showed me a different way of hunting. Walking through the woods, their dog would chase squirrels up the trees into holes that the squirrels used for nests. The teenage boys then cut some limber tree branches and trimmed off any side branches but left a fork at the end of their squirrel switch. One of them would climb the tree, and, when he was high enough, he would run the forked end of his switch into the hole. By twisting it, the squirrel's fur was wrapped around the switch, and the squirrel could be pulled out of the hole. The squirrel was then dropped down to the second boy who would finish it off with a quick blow to the head. That day ended with a sackful of squirrels, and a few went home with me to be cooked for supper.

One snowy day when the snow was nearly knee-deep, the same boys all showed up with their dachshund for a rabbit hunt. We went looking for brush piles, and, after we had encircled the brush piles, the dachshund was released to allow it to go into the brush piles to chase out the rabbits. Rabbits cannot run well in fresh deep snow. It was easy to chase down the rabbits and finish them with a blow to the head. Later, I found that rabbits couldn't run as fast as a person can in thick, tall, alfalfa; and that made it easy to catch rabbits from time to time in Dad's hay fields.

There was a tradition that when the first cold day arrived, it was announced that "It's hog-killing weather." After several phone calls, the next day people began to arrive with hogs in their wagons. The previous owners had built a rack with pulleys that could be used to lift hogs. There was also a large metal tub, to be filled with boiling water for the purpose of loosening the hair from the hide of the hogs as soon as the hogs had been killed. It sounds strange, but a hog-killing was a huge social event enjoyed by everyone. The wives all brought food and prepared a big spread, while the men killed and butchered the hogs and some of the women kept wood fires going under huge iron pots where the skins and fat were boiled. The resulting grease was ladled into buckets to cool and to make lard for cooking. Some of the men coated hams with brown sugar and salt and then hung those in our smokehouse. The kids ate the freshly cooked pork skins and played. All in all, a hog-killing was the best event of the year.

One very cold winter day, I fell for one of the world's oldest pranks. As we were walking past a metal gatepost, A. J. asked me what frost tasted like. When I confessed that I didn't know, he suggested that I lick some of it off that metal post. Instantly, my wet tongue froze to the pipe. I don't know how long I was frozen to the pipe before the warmth of my tongue caused the ice to thaw and I was released, but I do know that I never tried it again.

THE PAW PAW PATCH

A couple of years later, when it became apparent that a war in Korea was likely and that my father would be required to return to the bag plant in Indiana, my parents sold the farm in Kentucky and bought a farm in southern Indiana. That farm outside of Georgetown was close enough that it would be possible for Dad to commute to the bag plant and Mom would be close enough to Louisville, Kentucky, so she could work there if she chose to. That farm would also put my sister, Barbara, and me closer to our maternal grandparents. Even though he had never served in the Armed Forces, Dad's earlier role in the defense plant put him in a critical knowledge category; the government could require him to return to work in the event of a war. As expected, the Korean War did break out. Dad soon had the dual responsibilities of milking cows each morning and evening and of working at the bag plant five days each week.

While living on that farm, I had a few chores. The enjoyable chores were feeding the calves and hogs. A less enjoyable job was shoveling the manure out of the milking parlor each morning and evening after the cows were milked. None of the chores took very long; there was plenty of time to look for fun wherever fun was to be had. My little sister was often around, so, as big brothers do, I found ways to aggravate her. My favorite way was to fill a shovel with manure and chase her around the barn threatening to throw it on her. I thought it was great fun, but I doubt that Barbara enjoyed the game as much as I did.

When corn was planted, pumpkin seeds were added in with the seed corn, and, by the time the corn was ready for picking, there were pumpkins scattered all through the cornfield. The pumpkins ended up as Jack-o'-lanterns, pumpkin pies, and hog feed. One day, Dad hooked the wagon to his tractor, and after we had a wagonful of pumpkins, we went to feed the hogs. In the process of picking corn, the tractor and wagon had run over many of the pumpkins. While we were throwing pumpkins to the hogs, a flock of Canadian geese flew over, circled the cornfield, and landed. I asked Dad if I could take his .22-caliber rifle to shoot a goose. To my disappointment, he told me that he sold the rifle because he was afraid that I would play with it and that someone might get shot. I decided that I was going to find a way to kill one of the geese and took off at a run toward the field. On the way, I looked for a stick or a rock. The world is covered with rocks and sticks, but when you need one, guess what, there won't be one.

Getting closer, I could tell that the geese had gathered around smashed pumpkins and were feeding on those. One pumpkin was right next to our garden, separated from it by a row of weeds and tall grass. Nothing else stood between the garden and the geese. With no weapon to be found, the next best idea seemed to be that of crawling along the edge of the garden until I was close enough to jump out and grab the nearest goose. Sneaking up quietly was easy for a small boy; I had a lot of practice from sneaking up on my father, and soon I was less than four feet from the nearest goose. A mighty leap got me over the weeds, and I was able to put both hands on the goose. The field exploded with squawking geese, and my goose got away. If I had caught him, what would he have done to me? Who would have had who?

During the time we lived in Indiana, Dad bought a TV. It was one of the first and had a small round screen. That was before there were colored movies, and all TV pictures were black and white. Ours was the first TV in that area and was the center of attention. One night a week, we would set up chairs to make a theater of the living room. Wrestling was the big attraction. Our neighbors came one night a week to cheer on whomever Gorgeous George was wrestling that night. Programming began about four o'clock in the afternoon when the test pattern went off and the *Howdy Doody* show came on. With only the news and one or two shows to watch, there was a lot of time to read; that was the beginning of a lifelong love of reading.

There was one boy, a couple of years younger than me, living on an adjacent farm. He loved my Dad and would come around as often as he could, more to be with Dad than with me. Even though he was younger than me, we spent many hours exploring the farm and picking every kind of berry and fruit that was available. The place had blackberries, dewberries, and raspberries in every gully and along every fence. The raspberries never made it back to the house; we ate every one of those we found. The real treat came when the paw paw trees would drop their fruit. The paw paw is the largest fruit occurring in the wild in this country, but that farm was the only place I have ever seen a paw paw tree. The fruit is delicious and tastes something like a sweet banana. I still dream of finding some ripe paw paws. Mom taught me a song that she had learned as a child. A portion of some unknown author's the song "Paw Paw Patch" is:

Where, oh where, oh where is Susie?
Where, oh where, oh where is Susie?
Where, oh where, oh where is Susie?
Way down yonder in the paw-paw patch.
Chorus:
Picking up paw-paws; put 'em in a basket.
Picking up paw-paws; put 'em in a basket.
Picking up paw-paws; put 'em in a basket.
Way down yonder in the paw-paw patch.

Around the house were peach trees, apple trees, cherry trees, and plum trees; there was almost always some treat to be found. Persimmon trees were scattered though the woods, and while a green persimmon is terrible, when the persimmons were ripe—usually with the first frost—they tasted great. We competed with the opossums and raccoons for persimmons, and while the animals got most, we managed to find and enjoy our share.

A treat that very few have experienced is the beechnut. A burr-like shell surrounds that little triangular nut, but it is easy to remove. Since beech trees were the most common trees in our woods, it was always worth the effort each fall to search for beechnuts. By the way, beechnuts taste nothing like Beechnut gum or Beechnut chewing tobacco.

Next to our driveway were several large black walnut trees. Walnuts have a thick husk that must be removed, and then the nuts have to be allowed to dry for a few weeks prior to cracking and removing the meat. Removing the husk is a nasty job, but I found an easy way. I would pick up and throw the walnuts into the part of our driveway that curved down a hill to the springhouse, where cans of fresh milk were chilled by spring water that ran into a concrete holding tank. Three days a week, a refrigerated truck from a dairy processing plant came to pick up our milk cans. The milk truck coming in and out of the farm ran over the walnuts and did a great job removing the husks. Cracking black walnuts is much harder than cracking English walnuts but is well worth the effort. Mom used those walnuts as topping on homemade ice cream and other deserts.

Most of what we ate came from the farm, and much of it was just there waiting for us to gather it. Bantam chickens had free run of the farm but usually stayed around the barn. Those are smaller than the much more common breeds of domestic chickens and thrive on being allowed to roam free. They roosted in trees and made their nests in the areas of tall grass around fences and trees. One of my tasks was to locate the nests to place a fake wooden egg in each of the nests to fool the hens into thinking that there were only one or two eggs. With that done, the hens would continue laying eggs rather than setting and hatching baby chicks. We would gather their fresh eggs each day, but after quite a few weeks, I would be instructed to leave a certain nest alone, to allow that mother hen to raise a flock. We always had eggs and chickens to eat and never really had to work at it. Mom was great at fixing deserts, and, with a surplus of eggs, milk, and fruits, we had custards, pies, and cobblers almost every day.

SUPERMAN

Christmas was always an exciting time. The first part of the process of preparing for Christmas was to make the decorations. Mom taught us to use a needle and threads to string popcorn, to make ropes to wrap around the Christmas tree, and to make our own ornaments. Some were made by cutting out paper and gluing it to make three-dimensional stars, and some were things we made of paper mache. In those days, the school spent weeks preparing for the Christmas presentation. I can't sing a note, but even I had a small solo to sing. Preparing for Christmas meant spending a morning searching for the right Christmas tree. The perfect tree had to be there on the farm somewhere, so Dad and I had to find it. After searching the entire farm, we managed to find the one perfect tree each year. With the right tree in the house, the decorating began in earnest. With the passage of each day, there was more and more excitement. It seemed that the days just would not pass soon enough, as we looked forward to finally seeing presents around the tree.

By the time I was in the fourth grade, there was no doubt that Santa Claus was just a fairy tale and that he was not real; I knew it, and so did all my friends—well, at least, until that one Christmas Eve. My sister and I were both sick. When Mom and Dad went to the barn to milk the cows, the two of us resurrected, and that was our opportunity to jump up and down on the sofa. After tiring out, we quieted down while our parents were at the barn, milking. I still remember quite vividly that I was lying down on the couch and Barbara was curled up in a big comfy stuffed chair. We went to sleep, and, when I woke up, there were presents around the tree. I grabbed Barbara, and the two of us ran to the barn to tell Mom and Dad that Santa had come. They were still milking the cows, but, after some begging and pleading, Mom agreed to come with us to see what Santa had left. For the next two or three years, I would pretend that I knew better than to believe in Santa, but deep down I knew Santa was real. After having six children of my own and spending many hours assembling toys on Christmas Eve, I still sometimes wonder if Santa Claus did come that night.

Looking back at those years, it is obvious that God was at work in my life. He had given me wonderful parents and was continually protecting me. Years later when I think of friends who died young, I wonder why He allowed those to die and not me. I had a vague sense that there was a God, but that was as far as I went with that thought. I know that He had to have been with me as I decided to follow my imagination and be like Superman. One afternoon, when I was wearing my favorite T-shirt—a blue one with the big red letter "S" on the chest—I pinned a towel on the back to make a cape like Superman's. I climbed up a tree and jumped down onto the roof of the garage. After reaching the peak of the garage, it was time, so with outstretched arms I dived off. Superman flew, but David Roberts did not. The big red S stood for "Stupid," not "Superman." I did manage to survive without any injuries.

Sometime later, we all went to see the famous Barnum and Bailey Circus when it came to Louisville. Of all the things that impressed me, the thing that impressed me most was the high-wire act. When I got home, I laid out a rope on the grass and found that I could walk on it. The next day, I decided that if an expert could walk on a tight rope or a wire, then I could walk on a board fence. The best fence for walking on had to be the four-plank fence next to the milk shed, or the springhouse, where the cans of fresh milk were kept. Climbing up on the milk shed was easy, and from there I stepped over onto the top plank. I was doing great for almost one step, until I fell across the top plank, landing on my chest. I hit the ground, unable to breathe, and in pain worse than anything I had ever felt before. Eventually, I could breathe, and though I hurt, I never told my parents about my injury or about trying to become a circus performer. I still have a lump on my chest from where that fracture healed.

While on that farm, I came to know a lot of others my age, and we managed to find plenty of opportunities to pull pranks. Our best pranks were those we dreamed up to play when kids came from Louisville with their parents. There were three pranks that always worked. My friends and I would take off our shoes so we could convince our unsuspecting visitors that country kids always went barefooted. Soon, we would engage our visitors in a game where we would blindfold them, turn them around three times, and bet them that they couldn't go touch one particular person just by picking out the right voice. The right one of us would stand behind a fresh wet cow pie, and each of us would whisper something. The visitor would then head straight toward the spot where he had heard and identified the correct person's whisper, and would, of course, step in the fresh cow pie.

After recovering from his surprise, the suspicious visitor would clean up and reluctantly decide to go with us to check out the woods. On the way, we would take them through a field that had an electric fence. Electric fences are not dangerous but can give out a pretty good shock. My friends and I would walk up to the fence; even though we knew we would get a shock, we would grab the wire and step over the fence. The unsuspecting visitor, having seen that everything was okay, would then step up and grab the electric fence wire, usually letting out a yell. Our guest would realize that he had been tricked but would forgive us and continue with us into the woods.

There were always some big anthills to use for one more prank. As we walked through the woods, we would talk about stopping somewhere to rest and to decide where we wanted to go next. My country friends and I would quickly sit down on the ground in a circle, leaving one open spot—the spot where the anthill was located. Our visitor would always choose to join us and never failed to sit on the anthill. After jumping up, undressing and brushing off all the ants, our visitor was congratulated on having finishing his initiation, and we would encourage him to bring a friend the next time so that another city boy could officially become a farm boy.

Probably my worst prank involved the younger boy from the adjacent farm. He was a very good kid and loved my father. The only problem was that he never learned to speak softly. Every time he opened his mouth, it was with a loud high-pitched voice. In an effort to calm the cows, there would be soft music playing on a radio in the milking parlor. When the cows came into the milking parlor, there would be ground corn for them to eat, and the milking process would begin. I learned later that cows and other mammals, including nursing mothers, all have what is called the "milk let-down reflex," which requires that they be relaxed.

Anything that causes anxiety or startles them will result in an immediate and nearly complete cessation of milk flow. When Dad realized that his cows would stop giving milk every time the neighbor boy showed up, Dad told him many times that he was to stay out of the barn.

We had one very nervous cow that would immediately raise her tail and spray the area with liquid stool if anything startled her. Hoping that if he gave her plenty to eat and milked her first and let her leave the barn he could avoid having a mess to clean up, that cow always got preferential treatment. One day, as Dad was putting the cows in the milking stalls, the boy showed up. I stood outside the barn with him, and, just as Dad was hooking up the teat cups of the milking machine to the first cow, I told my little friend to go in quietly, sit down, and ask my Dad a couple of questions. That poor kid walked in, sat down behind the cow with his feet in the gutter, and blurted out, "Mr. Roberts!" Never in my life have I seen such a mess. I probably should have been ashamed, but, at that age, I just laughed. At least, we had a hose to wash him off.

SPITBALL

Georgetown High School and the elementary school had a combined enrollment of about two hundred students. The fourth and fifth grades were enjoyable, and I learned some important lessons there. One day, as we were coming back from recess, I saw someone—who I thought was a friend—bent over, tying his shoe. I was greatly mistaken. My friend's mother had dressed her two sons alike that day. One was in the fourth grade with me, and one was in the eighth grade. The person tying his shoes was the older brother. I realized which of the two brothers I was looking at right after I ran up and goosed him. It was a hard lesson I learned that day: it is not a good idea to goose someone twice your size.

The last day of school at the end of my fourth grade school year, I was sitting very near the first baseline during a high school baseball game when I turned to talk with someone sitting on my right. Suddenly, someone yelled, "Look out," and I turned just in time to catch a foul ball with my mouth. Every tooth in my mouth was knocked loose; fortunately, I did not loose any. My only meals for more than a month that summer were milk shakes and whatever else that I could drink through a straw. I learned a life lesson that day: keep your eye on the ball.

For several years, I had worked at perfecting the process of making spitballs, perfecting my aim, and shooting spitballs through a straw. The fifth grade began with a new teacher, one new to me and to the school. After the bell rang, this big burly man got up, walked to the blackboard, and began to write his name. As he was writing, I stood up, fired my spitball, and stuck it to the blackboard right in the middle of his handwritten, "Mr..." Our new teacher glanced over his shoulder and continued to write his name. He then sat down, told us his name and that he had just moved to Georgetown to be closer to some of his family. He told us that he thought he would like Georgetown and that he hoped that he would soon make some new friends. Then came the chilling words, "I was walking down the street yesterday and met a friend from back in the days when I was coaching college football at Western Kentucky Teacher's College. My old friend told me that I would be teaching his son and said that if his son ever misbehaved, I should make an example out of him. It sure was good to see Luke Roberts again. David, come up here!" I knew that I was in big trouble. He had a big wooden paddle with holes drilled in it, and he knew how to use it. Everyone in that class, particularly me, learned to behave that day. I was afraid to tell my parents what had happened and kept it a secret, until Dad was about eighty-one years old when I thought it might finally be safe to tell him.

Actually, not everything I did was bad. Now, I not only love animals but they also seem to be drawn to me. One enjoyable activity was making pets of as many animals as possible. I made it my goal to befriend a cottontail rabbit that hung out around a toolshed. By sitting quietly every evening with either a carrot or with apple slices in my hand, the goal was reached when my little bunny finally began to eat out of my hand. The next goal was to see if I could train our three pet goats to perform tricks. People were always amazed to see those goats walk on their back legs, roll over, and play dead on command.

Chickens, geese, pigs, and our cats were just not interested in learning any tricks, but our cows and calves were, at least, willing to become pets and soon learned to lie down on command. The cows were even willing to allow me to ride them bareback. Dad appreciated my efforts. From time to time, he would have someone come by, wanting to buy one of our dairy cows. Everyone in the dairy business really appreciates cows that are gentle. Dad would take the potential buyer out to look at the cows, and, when one was selected, he would tell that cow to lie down. He would then walk over, sit down on the cow, and negotiate a price. He could usually sell that cow for a premium.

At some point, Mom and Dad realized that once the expected war in Korea began, it would be best that we moved to Louisville, Kentucky. Moving would offer her an opportunity to earn a degree in accounting by going to college at night, and she could more easily begin working again. The farm was put up for sale, and, knowing that we would be moving, Mom found a job with Aetna Oil Company in Louisville, Kentucky, and began commuting. That worked out relatively well, since my school in Georgetown, Indiana, was only about one block from where some friends lived, making it possible for Barbara to stay with them during the day and for me to come from school to stay there until Mom could pick me up on her way home.

While we lived in the country, my best friend was our dog, Potty. She was not a friend only to me but was also invaluable to my dad. Milking cows requires that they be brought in from the pastures and put in the barn, at least, twice a day. Rather than walking all over the farm to gather the cows, Dad would get up each morning, walk into the kitchen, open the door, and say, "Get 'em." When he had eaten breakfast, he would head to the barn, knowing that the cows would be there. Potty would have covered the entire farm, gathered the cows, and would have every one of them in the barn. Then, before the evening milking, Potty would repeat the process.

There is no way Dad could have assigned a value to all the work done by that dog. After the Korean War started, Dad was called back to work at the bag plant. It was too demanding to try to continue managing a dairy farm while working five days a week at the plant. After selling the farm, all of us regretfully decided it would be better to leave Potty with the new owner on the farm where she could live out her life doing what she loved—herding cows.

RESTRICTION

As soon as the school year ended, with the farm sold, we moved to Louisville, Kentucky, where I started the sixth grade. Dad was working at the bag plant; Mom was working as the secretary to the President of Aetna Oil Company and wanted to start night classes at the University of Louisville. Prior to moving, our parents spent a lot of time talking with my grandmother, Cora, who was known by everyone as Granny, and her second husband, Russell Jackson or Jack, a quiet man who had been a newspaper reporter before becoming a taxi driver. Everyone agreed that it would be good for Granny and Jack to sell their house and move in with us. That really did work out well, and Granny was a hit with all of the kids in the neighborhood. Many times, there would be a knock at the back door, and some child would ask, "Can I come play with Granny?" I was always at ease around Jack, and he soon became my confidant. Later on, he volunteered to teach me to drive; learning to drive was a pleasure, I could always feel relaxed with him teaching me.

That first summer in Louisville was less enjoyable than it should have been, even though on our street there were four other boys my age who quickly became good friends. Most of those friendships have lasted for the rest of our lives. In another neighborhood, there were several boys who tried to start fights whenever they passed through our neighborhood. One of them said something to me one day, and a fight ensued. My mother, looking out a window, saw it and came running to break up the fight. I was scolded, and she told me that if I ever got in another fight, she was going to punish me with two weeks of restriction. Sure enough, a few days later, the same boy came by, and I ran out and jumped him. That earned me two weeks of restriction; I was not to set foot outside of our house and yard. My newly found adversary heard that I was restricted to our house and yard, so he came by to taunt me as he rode his bicycle in circles just far enough out in the street to be beyond my reach. He finally rode by close enough for me to reach him and pull him off his bike. When he landed in our yard, I jumped on him. Once again, Mom was watching through the front door. She gave me the original two weeks restriction plus six more weeks of restriction. I was not being allowed to leave the house or have any visitors for six weeks. As you might imagine, there was plenty of time to read, and I read so many books that it was all my parents could do to keep me supplied.

My grandfather, Fred Burden, Granny's first husband, heard of my restriction and loved the story; he bought me two pairs of large bulky boxing gloves for my birthday. My friends and I were instructed that whenever any of us had a disagreement, the situation was to be resolved by boxing. We had a number of such matches, but we all learned that fighting was really no fun, so we quit. About five years later, I was walking through a park and walked up on the same boy that I had pulled off of his bicycle. He was shocked to see me and pulled out his knife, and I realized that he was reacting in fear of another fight. After I assured him that I was not interested in causing any trouble, he put away his knife and left.

The sixth grade was spent learning nothing. The teacher did no teaching and, by the end of the school year, the administration fired him. After a year of learning essentially nothing and forgetting much of what I had previously learned, whenever I needed to write anything, I had always felt very inept.

All of us in that class waited out the weeks just looking forward to Christmas. That Christmas, Dad proved that he was a very wise father; he surprised me with a spinning rod, a Mitchell spinning reel, a tackle box, fishing lures, hooks, and sinkers. He also bought himself an identical outfit to use, at least, once a week when he took my friends and me fishing. During the summers, he took us with him on his way to work and would drop my friends and me off to fish. On his way home, Dad would join us to fish for a short while before heading home. When I was in high school, Dad bought a shotgun and told me that, if I could save up enough money to buy a shotgun, we could begin hunting. I saved a little money; ten dollars bought an old rusty single-shot Sears brand shotgun without a firing pin. I made a firing pin from a nail, and we began to hunt rabbits. I am sure that Mom, Granny, Jack, and Barbara got tired of seeing fish and rabbits on the table, but Dad and I enjoyed them. Later, when I was in medical school, I realized that I had made it through junior high, high school, and college without getting in trouble, not because I was naturally good but because I was too busy fishing and hunting to get in trouble.

At the age of eleven, someone invited me to go with him to a nearby Methodist church. I continued attending church, up until college when going to church just didn't seem very important. For a while, I believed that God would want me to become a minister of some sort, but as I watched the pastor of that church, I knew that growing up to be a boring and stiff old man held no attraction. For more than sixty years, I have carried the thought that maybe the ministry was to be my career, but really there is no doubt that I was born to follow Dr. Plumlee in a medical career. At the age of twelve, we were all told that we should go through a confirmation class and ceremony. Everyone else did, but to me it seemed to be a waste of time. On the day of confirmation, my dad and I went fishing.

Before our family moved to Louisville, public transportation was an important consideration, as they wanted their children to be able to easily travel to the main library, swimming pools, and schools. They bought a house on a street named Eagle Pass, which ran through an area known as Audubon Park, named after the artist John J. Audubon. Louisville had excellent public transportation; there were two bus transit lines that serviced our neighborhood. One of the services had a bus stop only half a block from our house, next to the street sign and a streetlight. On at least three occasions, the streetlight burned out; each time during the night, the street sign underwent a minor change. Someone painted out the letter P in "Eagle Pass." Normally, the sign would not be repainted for, at least, two weeks, and the altered name was a source of amusement for those passing by. For some reason, my parents always thought they knew the name of the culprit.

THE RED CIRCLE

Junior high school included the seventh grade through the ninth grade. Most of those years were relatively uneventful. I generally tried to do my best in most subjects—that is, except for the first grading period in English. With fear and the expectation of punishment, I brought home my first report card of the year with a D- in English. My parents took me to the kitchen to sit down and talk with them. To my surprise, their response was to offer me the opportunity to earn a new bicycle. All I had to do was to get an A+ in English on my next report card. That next grading period, I worked as hard as I could; the teacher allowed me to read three extra books in order to give extra credit for book reports. I was proud to show off my A+, and then even more proud of my new 3-speed Schwinn bike.

My favorite teacher was Mr. Merriman, my ninth grade science teacher. As the year drew to an end, my grades were great, but my behavior in his class slipped; in fact, it was pretty terrible. At that school, a circle around a grade indicated bad behavior. I suppose most parents were aware of that, but mine didn't know, and I certainly didn't tell them. When I showed off my report card with a big red circle around an A+, Mom was so proud. She assumed that her son was a great student and that the teacher wanted to emphasize that by putting a big red circle around the grade. I never told her the truth.

PRESENT! ARMS!

By the end of junior high school, I knew that I wanted to be a part of the ROTC in high school. Louisville Male High School, an all boys' school, was the only high school in Louisville with a college preparatory curriculum and was the only school with an ROTC program. I begged my parents to help me get into Male High. That school was the oldest high school west of the Allegheny Mountains, established in 1856. and was an all boys' school.

Later, an all girls' school had been established and named Louisville Girls High School. Though I lived outside their district, the school district policy was to allow students who wanted the college preparatory curriculum or the ROTC program to attend Male High School. I signed up for both the college preparatory program and for the army ROTC. I knew that I wanted to go to the US Military Academy in West Point, New York; Male High was perfect for me.

That summer, before school started, the big news was that Louisville Male High School and Louisville Girls High School would be merged and the school would be known as Louisville Male and Girls High School. The Male High School paper was the *Brook N Breck,* so named because the school was located at the corner of Brook and Breckinridge Streets. During my senior year, I was the editorial writer of the school paper. Our principal, Mr. Milburn, gave permission to the student staff to focus on an effort to change name of the school. Each month, we ran an editorial calling for a name change, pointing out that Louisville Male and Girls High School was a poor name, one not in keeping with the legacy of the school, and we mailed the paper to all of the alumni. By the end of my senior year, that hated name was changed back to Louisville Male High School. Everyone celebrated, including the girls.

At the beginning of my first year, as a sophomore weighing ninety-two pounds and being five feet two inches tall, I was easily intimidated. By the end of my sophomore year, I weighed two hundred and nine pounds, was six feet tall, and arrogant. My rapid rate of growth made my parents glad that I was in an ROTC program where uniforms were supplied to the cadets. About every six weeks, all of my now much too small uniforms were traded in, and a new set was taken home. I grew so fast that my parents were barely able to keep me supplied with shoes and clothes for the days that I didn't wear uniforms. The uniforms were standard army issue khaki uniforms that were to be starched and ironed.

I have to thank the ROTC and Granny for teaching me the art of ironing clothes. Granny did most of the housework and cooking, since Mom was working and going to school at night. Those students in the Honor Guard always wore their uniform shirts with military creases—three creases down the back and one crease down each side in the front. When I informed Granny that military creases would make my uniforms look much better, she agreed and walked away from the ironing board with the words, "Fine, you will certainly have nice-looking uniforms from now on out because you are going to be the one ironing your uniforms and all your clothes." She would occasionally repent some and iron one of my non-uniform shirts.

I knew that I wanted to try out for the Honor Guard drill team and knew that practicing the manual of arms and some of the special routines at home would be helpful. The NRA was selling military surplus World War I bolt-action O3-A3 Springfield rifles for fourteen dollars. Since that was the type of rifle used by the drill team, Dad said he would help me order one. I had a little money saved from mowing yards and was excited when it was time to mail off my order for a Springfield rifle. The rifle came packed in a very thick rust protecting grease, Cosmoline, and removing it required about three days of work. For the next year, I practiced some complicated and slightly dangerous tricks with my rifle. The sharp, pointed blade front sight created a few small cuts but nothing much worse than scratches. Eventually, the hours of practice helped earn me a place in the Honor Guard. Years later, that rifle was used to kill my first eight-point buck.

Male High had a 250-piece, all male ROTC marching band that performed at all of its football games and marched in all of the parades. Usually, the Honor Guard also performed and always marched in every parade. In Louisville, the biggest parade is the Derby Parade, a part of all the celebrations surrounding the Kentucky Derby. No parade in Louisville is a parade, unless there are a lot of horses. Parades were a problem for those of us in the Honor Guard. As we marched, we would be continuously going through the manual of arms, along with a few trick routines. To get an audience's attention, we loosened the screws on our rifle stocks to ensure that each time we slapped the rifle stock as we went through the manual of arms, it would make a loud noise. Before marching in parades, we put metal taps on our heels so that those watching would hear each step and would hear us when we stopped and clicked our heels together.

Often, a part of our routines involved noisily slamming the rifle butt with its metal plate on the pavement as we marched. Since we always had several groups of riders on non-housebroken horses ahead of us, the streets were heavily littered with droppings. It never failed that, at some point, each of us would sink the butt of the rifle down into a pile of horse manure; usually that would happen, at least, two or three times in each parade. Bringing the rifle to either the right shoulder or left shoulder arms position required grabbing the manure-covered butt of our rifles. Eventually, each of us marched with a handful of manure at a measured fourteen inches from our noses. That smell would not leave me until I could get a bath.

During my junior and senior year, I usually rode with my father as he went to work each morning and had him drop me off at school about an hour and a half before school started. I had permission to go to the weight room for a workout in my effort to build up the strength that would be needed if I was accepted at West Point. I gave it my best and was certain that the United States Military Academy would be a part of my future.

A NEW VISION

In 1956, it was announced that the Louisville public schools would end racial segregation. As the summer drew to a close and the football team was involved in its pre-season practice, the team spread the word that we were to welcome any black students and that those playing football were "good guys."

A couple of days before school started, the newspaper and the local TV news programs made everyone aware that the Klu Klux Klan planned to picket Louisville Male High School to protest desecration. Everyone that I knew was angry that the KKK had picked our school out of all the schools in the country for their protest. As students began to talk, a plan of action was formulated: all the senior boys would bring bats, clubs, sticks, two-by-fours or something, and we were to spread out about three blocks from the school to wait for the opportunity to ambush the KKK. When the first day arrived, I got to school early to find that there were camera crews and trucks from all the major networks parked in front of the school. Apparently, the KKK got word of what was waiting for them; at least, they didn't show up, and school started without any problem.

During my senior year, three of us were rotated through the position of regimental commander and were given the rank of cadet colonel. By the time I became the regimental commander, I felt certain that I was prepared for the West Point. Even with everything else going on, I still managed to go fishing or hunting every Saturday and Sunday. Somehow, I kept my grades up enough to have a real chance of being accepted at West Point.

There was one other factor that made me absolutely certain that I could go to West Point. When my father was younger, he had known both the future Senator Albert Gore, Sr. of Tennessee and his wife Pauline. The three of them spent time together taking some summer courses in Madison, Wisconsin, and he had stayed in touch with them. As a boy living in the country outside of Georgetown, Indiana, I still remember Senator Gore and Mrs. Gore coming to visit and remember thinking that he didn't look like any one very special. When I started talking about going to West Point, my parents wrote to Senator Gore, who said that he would use one of his senatorial nominations to help me when I applied. Years later when their son was the vice president, I remembered the time Senator and Mrs. Al Gore, Sr. visited my parents and wondered why their son was not with them. Suddenly, the terrible truth hit me; he had not been born yet. That kind of realization will make you feel old.

Each January, Male High hosted the Louisville Invitational Tournament. On the first day of the tournament, our senior class students was allowed to spend the last couple of hours in the cafeteria where there would be representatives from a number of colleges, industries, and the military services. At the US Army table, there was a very knowledgeable sergeant who explained that it was the policy of all of the service academies not to accept anyone who required any visual correction. The greatest disappointment I had ever known was when he told me that I was not qualified for admission to West Point.

I left the cafeteria and walked to the gymnasium where the basketball tournament would soon be starting. I walked up the stairs and was standing behind the south end basket and watching someone run a dust mop over the gym floor when an ROTC instructor, Mr. Adams, a retired army major, walked up and put his hand on my shoulder to greet me. He leaned on the rail and asked, "What did you find out?" I explained that I would not be able to go to West Point because I wore glasses. His next question was, "What are you going to do?" When I told him that I would try to get a degree in engineering and then an army commission, he said, "Don't do that, you need to go to medical school, you'd make a good doctor." As he said that, he turned and walked off. Instantly, I remembered Mom telling me that I had been named after Dr. Plumlee. From that moment on, my career path was set: I would plan on going to medical school and would serve as a medical officer.

A short time later, Mr. Adams moved away from Louisville. I never saw him again and have often regretted that I never had the opportunity to tell him about the impact of that kind thought and his casual statement and how it changed my life. God had to have been at work that day as He guided me using Mr. Adams. I often think of how much a caring teacher can influence the life of a student. In fact, his statement resulted in me taking night classes every summer and every college semester. I wanted to get as many credits as possible, as quickly as possible; I determinedly set out on my new goal of going to medical school.

After finding that West Point was no longer an option, I became a little less concerned about having a perfect record.

One of the students had a very small car—a Crosley—and that car soon became the center of a prank. Six of us decided that we could bring it into the school and carry it up to the second floor to park it in front of the principal's office. We got it up there and stood with a crowd of students as we waited for Mr. Milburn, our principal, to arrive. Mr. Milburn was the coolest character I've ever met; he looked at the car as he calmly walked into his office and said, "Hmm, a Crosley." We expected something more to happen; we just didn't know how many pranks a principal of an all boys' school had endured. After that, we to took the car back down the stairs and back to where its owner had originally parked it.

That spring, the Billy Graham Crusade was to come to town. One of my church-going friends asked me to go to the Crusade with him one evening. That night, Freedom Hall, the coliseum at the Louisville Fairgrounds, was completely filled. I was really impressed when George Beverly Shea and an audience of twenty-six thousand people sang "How Great Thou Art." I can almost still hear it. When Billy Graham gave an invitation at the end of the sermon, my friend said, "We are supposed to go down." I went down and filled out a form, but I felt nothing and certainly did not make any commitment.

Graduation day brought with it the required practice at the Louisville Fair Grounds and Coliseum, where the ceremony would be held that evening. I drove there in Mom's new 1957 Desoto. That car had the big Hemi engine. No sixteen-year-old boy should ever be allowed to drive a car that powerful. After the practice session ended, someone asked me how fast the car could go. Several others challenged me to find out, and I accepted the challenge, not knowing that it would only be by God's grace that I would live another five minutes. Behind the coliseum was a very large paved area where the state fair was held each year. I started the car and headed back behind the coliseum and watched the speedometer climb to 120 miles per hour. Just as it hit 120, some man drove his restored model T Ford out in front of me. I have no idea how we both avoided death that moment, but somehow the collision was avoided. Once again, I had been protected, and, for the first time, I realized that there had to be a God.

THE PHONE CALL

After their parents had died, my grandmother had helped raise two young nephews and a niece. After they were grown, all three of them considered our home as the gathering place for holidays. One of them, Roberta, known to everyone as Bert, moved with her husband, Tommy, and their children to Montague, Michigan. All of the Roberts family went to visit them and enjoy the area; for Dad and me, it was an opportunity to enjoy some great fishing. On that trip, Tommy and Bert asked me several times to get together with a girl who lived there and recommended that we go to get ice cream or see a movie. I responded by letting them know that I just wanted to fish and was not interested in any girl.

After graduating from high school, I was allowed to take the car and drive up to Michigan with my grandparents and my sister. While I was there, I spent as much time fishing as I possibly could. Once again, Tommy and Bert kept insisting that I meet the girl who lived just down the road, suggesting that we go to the Lake Michigan beach for a picnic, go for ice cream, or go to a movie. I kept insisting that I wanted to fish; they told me that I should take her fishing and that girls liked to fish too. I had never met a girl who liked to fish. I told them that I didn't want any girl messing up the fishing. I never got together with her and never did any of those things. I did drive back home with a lot of fish stories.

In 1961, while I was watching a TV program, the phone rang. It was Tommy and Bert calling to ask me if I was watching TV. I told them that I was and what I was watching. Tommy suggested that I might want to change channels to watch the Miss America contest, since Miss Michigan was one of the five finalists. Then he told me that the girl I had avoided was Miss Michigan. I watched as Nancy Anne Fleming, Miss Michigan, won the crown and became Miss America. I had, for two summers, successfully avoided ever having a date with the future Miss America. It may just be a better story this way; she became a Democrat.

COLLEGE

Though the Korean War truce was signed in 1953, our country remained on a warlike status for several more years as the Cold War began. At the time I was preparing for college, some defense industries scaled back; the bag plant ceased operation, and Dad began looking for work. I talked with both Mom and Dad about my college plans, but there really was not much to discuss; deciding was easy. I knew that, with our family's financial uncertainty, I should plan to avoid any unnecessary expenses.

Both of my parents had gone to the University of Louisville; I had been taking some classes at night and enjoyed being on campus there. I never even considered any other colleges; all my friends were in Louisville, and I really wanted to go to medical school there. I did not need to consider a fraternity; home was still a great place to live, and I had more friends and activities than I had time. I enrolled, declared a pre-medical major, and joined the Air Force ROTC, since U of L did not have an Army ROTC program.

Soon after enrolling in college, Dad started working for the Kentucky Department of Revenue. Mom, who became a freshman at the University of Louisville at the age of fourteen, was now back in school making all A's and ready to help me set my course. She talked about the man that she thought was the best professor she had ever known, Morris Bein. She told me that I should try to sign up for his freshman English class; she said that he was demanding but that she had gotten an A back when she started her first year at U of L at the age of fourteen. On her strong recommendation, I made sure that I was enrolled in his English class.

After the first two weeks, I thought my mother hated me. I stayed with him for both semesters, but, for two semesters, I was sure that freshman English would kill me. On the last day of class, he told us that he wanted to discuss grades. Wallace Johnson was mentioned, and Mr. Bein said that he did not normally believe in giving anyone an A. He congratulated Wallace for doing an exceptionally good job and said that he believed Mr. Johnson was deserving and would be receiving an A-. He went on to tell us that he had only given one other person an A in more than thirty years of teaching and that the person he gave that grade to had been a student of his a good many years earlier. That A student was my mother. I was more relieved and happier with two Cs in English than I ever was for any A in any other class.

My trials with the English language were not over. I would say that English was my second language, but I don't have a first. My sophomore year was made much more difficult by the fact that a scientific writing course was required for pre-medical students. The course should have been easy, but I picked a subject for my term paper that was far too complicated for me. I picked the electrochemical process of anodizing aluminum as my subject. That might have been an easy subject for a chemical engineering student but not for someone who was focusing on biology. I asked the professor if I could change the subject for my term paper. She gave me the two unhappy options of either sticking with my original subject, or of writing not one but two term papers on two unrelated topics. I ended up writing a paper on stuttering and another on the subject of regeneration of amputated structures in reptiles. I was relieved when I could finally get back to the easy subjects of physics, math, comparative anatomy, German, and parasitology.

ELIZABETH TAYLOR

Other than my English classes, I enjoyed almost all of my classes and did well at the University of Louisville. The most enjoyment came from being in the Air Force ROTC. As a member of the ROTC, we wore our uniforms three days each week. In a psychology class, the professor was talking about peer pressure and the innate desire people have to look and dress the same as everyone else. At that point, he looked at me and told the class that I was an example, as I was wearing a uniform. He was at a loss for words when I pointed out that I was the only one in a uniform and that I should be complimented for my willingness to stand out from everyone else. I became the commander of the Honor Guard and the commander of the Color Guard.

In 1957, the year I graduated from high school, the Louisville newspaper, the *Courier-Journal*, was full of stories about the filming of the movie, *Raintree County*. The movie was being filmed in Kentucky and would star Elizabeth Taylor, Eva Marie Saint, Montgomery Clift, and Lee Marvin. Nearly every day there was an article about Elizabeth Taylor, who was called the most beautiful woman alive. There was a feature article in the Sunday magazine section that gave details about how she cared for her hair, even listing the number of strokes that she used each morning when she brushed her hair.

Not long after starting my freshman year, excitement began to build when it was announced that the world premier of the movie would be at the Brown Theater in Louisville. Plans included a number of balls and a parade. Then, best of all, we were told that the University of Louisville Air Force ROTC Color Guard would present the colors, the American Flag and the Commonwealth of Kentucky"s flag, when the National Anthem was performed at the start of the ceremony. I had read most of the articles about Elizabeth Taylor and the other stars and hoped that I might get to see them.

On the morning of the premier, we went to the theater for a run-through and to learn about the details of the opening ceremony. A large stage had been built in front of the theater. We were surprised to find out that we would not be marching away after the national anthem, as was the usual case. The person in charge told us that the ceremony would be on TV and would be filmed for use in newsreels. He wanted us to remain on the stage as a colorful background and said that as the producer, director, and the celebrities were introduced, they would line up on the stage in front of the color guard. When I looked over the stage, I saw that there were names taped to the floor to make sure that each person knew where he or she was to stand. Wow, I would get to see Elizabeth Taylor.

That evening, on cue, we marched up onto the stage, presented the colors, and took our position. As the program progressed, the dignitaries, producer, director, and the celebrities were introduced. I could not believe it when Elizabeth Taylor and her third husband, Mike Todd, the producer of the Academy Award movie *Around the World in 80 Days*, took their position directly in front of me. I was less than two feet from them. Next to them was Eva

Marie Saint. As the program went on, Elizabeth Taylor began berating her husband and everyone else using the most profane language I have ever heard. I was totally disgusted. When the ceremony finished, a very sweet and kind Eva Marie Saint came over and spent a minute talking to us and thanking us. I swore that I would never go to an Elizabeth Taylor movie.

In 1966, Richard Burton and Elizabeth Taylor appeared in the film, *Who's Afraid of Virginia Woolf?* Since Elizabeth Taylor had won the Academy Award in that movie, I decided that I would give her the benefit of the doubt and go to see the movie. Elizabeth Taylor played the vulgar, bitter wife of a college professor. After about ten minutes, I had seen and heard enough and left. My thought was that Elizabeth Taylor wasn't acting; she was just being the same Elizabeth Taylor that I had seen at the Brown Theater.

When the premier was over, it was back to a more routine life. Classes and labs took up most of my days, and homework controlled the nights. The Navy ROTC Color Guard and the Air Force ROTC Color Guard were very active in presenting the colors for the national anthem at home football and basketball games. The great thing about being on the Color Guard was that each of us was given two reserved seat tickets for the games, even for the NCAA championship tournament. It was particularly rewarding to get two tickets to watch the University of Louisville play in the final four. Reserved seats impressed girls—a great reason to be in the Color Guard.

THE INTERVIEW

College taught me that I was not cut out to be a gambler. My comparative anatomy class laboratory lasted almost four hours; at some point, my laboratory partner and I would break and go to the cafeteria for coffee. Each time, we utilized a coin toss to decide who would pay. For the entire semester, I lost every time. We agreed to use my coin, and I still lost every time.

Once again, there was an occasion when I could have easily been killed but unexplainably escaped harm. One pleasant day in May, after going out on a date, we were on the way back to her parent's house. It was a comfortable evening and perfect for driving with the windows open. The drive to her house was along a street that had a very tight S-shaped curve with a four-way stop at the end of the second curve. As we approached the first curve, I heard the sound of tires squealing and heard the roar of a car's engine; the sound seemed to be coming from the area of the intersection. Without thinking, I stopped. At that moment, a car came around the curve just ahead of us and began spinning, coming to a stop inches away from our car. The visibly shaken teenage boy sat in his car while I backed up to give him room; after he got his car straightened out, we drove on. If the windows had been rolled up, we might not have heard his car, and, if I had not stopped, we would have been in a serious accident. I confessed to her that I couldn't explain why I had stopped. Again, I either had to be incredibly lucky that night, or God had stepped in to protect us.

Each summer, I worked to help cover some of the costs of school by working at labor intensive jobs, which convinced me that I needed to finish my education. I worked at the Paramount Foods plant where one of the many tasks was unloading several truckloads of cucumbers each day and at the Aetna Oil Company warehouse loading and unloading trucks; I worked for Mattingly Construction Company as a truck driver. The job of truck driver sounded like a cushy job, but, after I started, I found out that driving was the easy part, and that loading and unloading was the hard part.

The first day on the job, I was asked if I could drive a dump truck, and I answered, "Yes." I was not asked whether or not I knew how to drive a dump truck. The owner of the company told me to take a shovel and a sledgehammer and sent me to a job site to break up a porch and take it to the dump. Leaving the office, I found that I could make the truck go where it was supposed to go and that I could figure out how to shift through all the gears. With that accomplished, a cold Coca Cola sounded like a good idea. I pulled off the road into a dilapidated filling station with a soft drink machine. The truck did not have seat belts and apparently did not have any shock absorbers. When I hit a pothole, the truck bounced so hard that I was thrown to the passenger's side, and the truck was without a driver. Somehow, I got back behind the steering wheel and managed not to hit anything. With a drink in my hand and some new knowledge about dump trucks, I drove to the job site.

When concrete steps and porches are poured, usually a wall is poured first and, after the wall has hardened, the area behind the wall is then filled in with dirt. The porch is then capped off with a slab of concrete, and the steps are poured. What everyone back at the construction company knew was that this particular porch and steps had been poured as one solid, three feet tall piece of concrete. I had been sent out with only a sledgehammer and a shovel as a test of character. When about eight hours had passed, the porch was broken up, and all that broken concrete was loaded and taken to the dump. I made it back a little after closing time. When I drove in, all the men were waiting for me, laughing. They all knew that a jackhammer was needed, but they had sent me to do the job with a sledgehammer and were waiting to see if I had passed their test. After shaking my hand, all of us went to the restaurant next door where I was treated to a cheeseburger, fries, a coke, and a lot of funny stories.

After each of those summer jobs, I was even more certain that I wanted to finish my education. Coming home from work each day, hot and sweaty, I would bathe, and, as soon as I had eaten, I would head for the campus and night classes. It was apparent that there was a difference in the students who attended night classes and those in my daytime classes. The night school students wanted to be there and were committed; too many of the day students were only there because their parents sent them. In the last few years, I have taught college classes and have realized that, for the most part, when you look at the new students in your class, the ones with the gray hair will be the ones who get an A. They know why they are there.

By the end of my junior year, only a few more credit hours would be needed to graduate. Medical schools were known to accept a few students after only three years of college. It seemed to be worth a try, so I applied for admission to the University of Louisville School of Medicine, where I could possibly finish my bachelor's degree while working on an MD degree. At that time, I was in the advanced ROTC program and scheduled to go to summer camp in San Antonio, Texas, between my junior and senior year. The days passed, and finally I got a letter that did not have the expected denial; instead, there was a date and a time for an interview. Needless to say, my family and I were excited.

The interview was with Dr. Arch Cole, the gross anatomy professor who was feared by most medical students. Filled with anxiety, I went in and sat down to face my interviewer. The first words out of his mouth were, "You are only eighteen, what were you thinking and what gave you the audacity to even apply for admission to a medical school?"

I gave him the only answer I could think of, "I couldn't get admitted if I didn't apply."

Then he asked, "Why is this the only medical school that you applied to?"

I couldn't think of a good answer but gave the only possible one. "This is where I want to go to medical school."

The next question was the one I feared. "If you can get A's in just about everything else, why did you get Cs in English?"

With my heart pounding and my palms sweating, I told him, "I'm terrible in English and had to work really hard to just to get that grade."

Then he asked me one more question, "What are you going to do if you are not admitted?"

I told him that I would reapply the next year and that if I still did not get admitted, I would become an officer in the Air Force. Dr. Cole said that I had done extremely well on the MCAT, the Medical College Admission Test, and he thought I would probably be accepted, but it might be necessary to wait another year.

Weeks passed, and the semester was drawing to an end when I went to pick up my gear for ROTC summer camp. As I got home and drove up the driveway, I could see Granny standing in the door holding a letter. It was my letter of acceptance. I was going to medical school. After hugging her, I drove back to the campus and turned in my gear while being congratulated by the entire ROTC faculty. They said to keep my uniforms and that they would use me as a backup member of the Color Guard, even while I was in medical school. That was a real gift; I continued to go to some games in uniform and continued to get those reserve seat tickets. All those Air Force ROTC faculty and staff members have a warm place in my heart. Their kindness sealed my commitment to the idea of becoming a doctor in the US Air Force.

A BOX OF BONES

A few days after my nineteenth birthday, along with a number of other students, we walked up the stairs through the doors and down the hall of the old stone building of the University of Louisville School of Medicine, where we hoped to spend the next two of our four years of medical school. At the end of the hall, a sign greeted us, directing all freshmen students to the fourth floor lecture room. Next to the elevator, another sign instructed us that students were not allowed to use the elevator. After settling down in the lecture hall at exactly eight o'clock in the morning, Dr. Arch Cole entered the room, and an assistant loudly closed the doors.

Dr. Cole began to speak and announced to everyone that he had not sent a taxicab to get us; we had asked to be there and had come of our own accord. He told us that all lectures would start on time and that no one would be allowed in after the doors had closed. He then told us that we would be expected to learn 2,500 new words during our first year. Next, we were told to look at the person on our left and the one on our right, because one of them would not be there at the end of the year. That statement was followed with directions to the dean's office, where we could go to withdraw and get a full refund of our tuition if we went there before noon. Three students got up and left immediately. With that, the lights went out, slides came up on a screen, and the lecture began.

After the lecture, we were directed to the gross anatomy lab to be divided into groups of four and sent to our assigned dissection table. There we met our cadaver. At the end of our first morning of dissection, we signed for a wooden box, which we were to take home and keep until the end of the course. That box was filled with bones, a complete skeleton.

Everyone knows that medical school is difficult and requires intensive studying. Never had I studied as hard as I did that first week. Sure that I was prepared, I faced my first written quiz the next Monday morning. The next day, our quizzes were returned, and mine had a grade of 65 percent. That was the day when all of us found out how hard we would have to study. I left school that day, wondering if applying for medical school was a mistake. From then on, all of my grades were much better, but the idea of having any spare time was gone.

Everyone either loved or hated Dr. Cole. No other professor was as demanding as he, but no other professor ever gave as much of himself to his students. Students were allowed to return to the gross anatomy lab each evening after classes and on the weekends. Dr. Cole would return each evening and would stay until late in the night to help any student who needed help. He also looked for good summer jobs for his students. He arranged jobs for Bert Sparrow and me at the Army Medical Research Laboratory on Fort Knox. He also referred three of us to the Veteran's Administration Hospital where we would begin covering the laboratory and X-ray departments at night and on weekends; the time at the VA hospital was educational, but we received no pay.

The anatomy laboratory exams were stressful. An anatomical specimen was placed at each table with some structure tagged. One minute was allowed for students to look at the specimen before a buzzer sounded. When the time expired, the student had to move to the next table. One of my classmates wanted to look at the other side of a specimen but was so nervous that he couldn't think to turn the specimen; he crawled under the table to look at the specimen from the other side.

To a great extent, the legendary fear of Dr. Cole was a creation of second year students, who tried their best to scare new freshman students. We were told tales about the terrible written and practical exams. They made sure we knew that we would probably fail the test on the brachial plexus. The brachial plexus is made up of the fifth through eighth cervical nerves and the first thoracic nerve. Those nerves come from the spinal cord and exit between the neck bones and the upper thoracic backbones, join and divide, encircle the large arteries and veins behind the collarbone, only to divide again before reaching and innervating muscles of the arm, hand, and chest. Those nerves also carry sensory impulses back to the spinal cord. Knowing that the brachial plexus exam would be the most difficult exam we would face, I tried to think of a way to learn all that information and soon realized that there was a way. I spent about half of one Saturday drawing the brachial plexus and listing all of the details on a poster board. For the next three months, that poster board was taped to the wall in front of my commode where it would be studied, at least once a day. My plan worked, and I managed to get a perfect grade on that exam.

Another exam that everyone feared was the laboratory practical exam on the wrist and hand. There are eight small bones in the wrist. Dr. Cole was known to have boxes covered with black cloth, with each containing a wrist bone hanging down by a string. It was possible to reach in to feel the bone, but the bone could not be seen. When we walked in for that test, there were the black boxes; we were expected to identify each of the bones by feel, to name the bones and state whether the bone in question was from the right or left side.

Every morning, Dr. Cole, a short man with a mustache, visited each laboratory table and would ask questions of each of the four students in turn. The questions would be increasingly difficult, and Dr. Cole would continue until the student could not answer. Once a student gave an incorrect answer, he would begin questioning the next student. After finishing with one group, he would move to the next table.

One day, a student left for a few minutes, returned, and asked one of his lab partners, "Has that little bastard come around yet?" As soon as the question was asked, the student realized that Dr. Cole was standing next to him. Dr. Cole questioned the other three and moved on to the next table. The rest of the semester, Dr. Cole would ask the other three questions and then move to the next table. He never spoke to or asked any questions of the one student. Each time there was a written test, Dr. Cole would grade every test, except that of the offending student. At the end of the course, Dr. Cole came around to speak to each student and let him or her know if they had received a passing grade. When he came to the table where the offensive question had been asked, he told three of the students they had passed and walked off. As he walked away, Dr. Cole turned around and said, "Oh, you can tell that little bastard he passed too."

Dr. Cole died in an automobile accident shortly after the end of my freshman year. I will never forget Dr. Arch Cole—he gave more of himself to his students than anyone could ever imagine. He was a legendary figure and the best professor I ever had.

WELL!

Eventually, the freshman year was finished. A number of students had dropped out of school, and about one third of the remaining class members had failed neuroanatomy; they had to spend their summer in Michigan, repeating the course in order to start the second year. Thankfully, that was not the case for Bert Sparrow or me. We had been recommended by Dr. Cole and were hired to work at the Army Medical Research Laboratory in Fort Knox, Kentucky. Two graduate psychology students were also hired to work on some projects. They would be working in a different building from the one Bert and I would be in. I had the smallest and most economical car. Four of us crowded into the tiny Anglia in order to save money on gas.

Bert and I were given some background information, and our jobs were outlined. After the first nuclear weapon test in 1945 and after dropping two atomic bombs on Japan, there had been numerous test blasts. In some of the tests, animals had been placed various distances from ground zero, but postmortem examinations had never been performed on any of the animals. Knowing that two medical students would be working in the veterinary pathology department, radiation dosimeters were surgically implanted into a number of dogs; those dogs were taken to a site, placed at differing distances from a radiation source, and exposed to radiation. When the dogs died, it was our job to do postmortem examinations on the dogs, collect specimens, and make microscopic tissue slides. Those specimens and slides would be archived for future study.

The exposed dogs soon began to succumb to the effects of radiation. Those that received higher levels of radiation exposure died first. The other animals continued to die at varying intervals, depending on the amount of radiation exposure. For a period of several weeks, we were doing postmortem examinations and collecting specimens for processing. The effects of radiation were devastating. Bert and I often wished that we could have brought in the leaders of all of the large nations to watch one of the postmortem examinations.

Eventually, the postmortem examinations were over with, and we began the process of embedding the specimens in paraffin using a microtome to cut the tissues microscopically thin and making thousands of stained slides. Bert and I were allowed to make up our own study sets, and we are probably the only two civilians with sets of slides made from postmortem examinations of animals exposed to radiation.

The four of us, Bert, the two psychology students, and I brought our lunch each day after we decided that there was really no good place to go for lunch. One of the two students always ate in his office, but the other—a very proper young lady—would frequently come to join us in the pathology department library. If she had not been such a lady, we probably would not have plotted to make her the subject for what we thought would be the perfect prank. Bert had heard of someone making a device that could create a sound much worse than that made by whoopee cushions. The device was made using a coat hanger, a button, and a rubber band. That night, when no one was looking, I cut a metal coat hanger and made it into the shape of a slingshot. Two ends of a cut rubber band could be threaded through two holes on one side of a button and back through the other two holes. The loose ends of the rubber band were tied together, and the loops on each side of the button were stretched over the slingshot-shaped device.

The next morning, we asked our young lady friend to come up and join us for lunch. Bert and I went into the library and sat down in the leather-cushioned chairs to practice the prank. I was to wind up the rubber band and place the device under my leg, and we were to wait for her to come in and sit down. Just as she was sitting down, I would lift my leg to allow the device to sound off, and then we were going to say, "Well," and get up to leave her sitting alone in the room. We practiced our prank twice, and the device worked perfectly.

As the time approached, I wound the device, put it under my leg, and we began our wait. Bert laughed first, and by the time we heard our friend walking down the hall, we were both laughing so hard that we were crying. When she stepped through the door with a quizzical look on her face, Bert and I were about to fall out of our chairs. I must have lifted my leg. A loud and very gross sound emanated from under my leg. She gave me a disgusted look, turned to walk out the door, and let out a loud, "Well!" On the ride back to Louisville, she never mentioned the event, but she never again came to eat lunch with us.

ONE FLOOR DOWN

When we started our second year in medical school, we moved down one floor; most of our classes were on the third floor, and a few were on the second. After spending the summer working in the veterinary pathology department at Fort Knox, I looked forward to starting our pathology class.

We were surprised when the chairman of the department, William Christopherson, MD, announced that we were to be a part of an experiment. When we were in the laboratory looking at slides of changes brought on by diseases, there would be instructors, but the instructors would not be allowed to answer any of our questions. All laboratory exams and written examinations would be returned to us without a grade and nothing to indicate whether or not we had answered questions correctly. At the end of the year, we would take a standardized test, one that is given to all medical students. The faculty wanted to compare our class to previous classes that had been taught using standard methods. None of us knew whether we had or had not learned anything. Apparently, I did reasonably well; I was offered a summer job in the Pathology Department of Louisville General Hospital.

The microbiology courses of bacteriology and tropical medicine seemed, in our minds, to move us from basic sciences into the applied science of medicine. One of the students asked the professor, since we would never encounter those conditions, why we were spending so much time on tropical diseases. The professor told us that someday we could find ourselves in Southeast Asia. We all laughed, since that was obviously not a possibility. A few years later, many of us spent a year or more in South Vietnam.

Bacteriology classes started at one o'clock in the afternoon. Usually, I brought a sandwich for lunch, but one day several of us went to a restaurant, ate a rather large meal, and returned for our bacteriology lecture. Our professor was covering something that wasn't holding my attention, and I began to doze. In the process, I yawned, and, at just that instant, an unexpected, very loud belch came out. With my mouth open wide, it was as if a megaphone was amplifying the sound. As our professor spun around in her effort to find the source, all of my classmates laughed and pointed toward me. Some friends they were.

The rest of the sophomore year went by without too much difficulty; a lot of study was required, but I enjoyed it. During that year, I worked at the VA Hospital every third weekend and two nights each week. The very first time that I was called to the X-ray department, a young man was brought down in a wheelchair with an order for a chest X-ray. Surprisingly, I recognized him as one of my classmates in high school. He recognized me and told me that he joined one of the military services after high school and that he had been given a medical discharge because of a melanoma. The X-ray demonstrated hundreds of metastatic nodules scattered throughout both lungs. After completing his X-rays, he asked if there was anything there. I couldn't bring myself to tell him what I had seen. I told him that I was not a radiologist and he would have to wait for his doctor to tell him about his radiology report. About a week later, he died.

Second year students were required to be on a call list to come in to Louisville General Hospital at night if there was an autopsy to be done. My first call left me feeling uneasy as I drove in. When I got there, they uncovered the body—the body of one of my professors, who had committed suicide. Medical school was becoming very real.

Between the second and third year, I worked on a research project in the Pathology Department. Most of the work involved giving several hundred white rats injections every day. Those rats had been injected with a cancer that could be transplanted from one rat to another. Half of the rats were given daily injections of normal saline; the other half were injected with an antigen that would hopefully cause them to develop an immune reaction and be cured of their cancer. The antigen did not result in the hoped-for cure. The two groups of rats were in separate rooms at the two different ends of a long hall.

One Monday morning, I came in to find that the group of rats that had been given the placebo, the normal saline, had all succumbed to an epidemic of pneumonia. The pneumonia was totally unrelated to the cancer, which was in an early stage. The professor who was heading up the study wrote a paper concluding that the antigen allowed rats with that cancer to live longer. He did not mention the pneumonia and the article was completely bogus, all just to have another article listed in his resume.

Sometime during my second summer break, I met and started dating a girl, who would later become my wife. Jackie Ochs was from a Lutheran family that would not allow me to continue to see her, if I wasn't a Lutheran. That problem seemed easy enough to solve; I read a small book, was baptized by sprinkling, and became a Lutheran. Her father was satisfied, and everyone thought it was great to have a medical student in his or her church. Being a Christian didn't bother me, I didn't break any rules, and I got to enjoy some nice covered dish lunches.

THE CLINICAL YEARS

The third and fourth years of medical school are called the clinical years. The majority of our time was spent in clinics, hospital wards, operating rooms, labor and delivery rooms, and emergency rooms. Lectures were given in hospital classrooms and occasionally in the big Louisville General Hospital amphitheater. I hope that there have been dramatic changes since my days there in the early 1960s.

Louisville General Hospital was a large city/county charity hospital with excellent surgical facilities. The labor and delivery units were very nice, as was the emergency care facility. The fourth floor was a world unto itself; it seemed to have been forgotten by those in the hospital's administration. Each of the four medical wards was a forty-bed open ward. Next to the nurses' station was a room with four beds for the most critical patients. At night, none of the forty bed units had a nurse; the only staffing consisted of one nursing student. One registered nurse supervised the entire fourth floor and up to 176 patients. Junior and senior medical students, interns, and resident physicians worked with the one nursing student to provide for the needs of the patients. That system worked but certainly would be considered archaic today.

From the first grade on, studying was something necessary; passing depended on it. Once I reached the clinical years, I couldn't quit reading and studying. No novel could ever have interested me as much as my textbooks on obstetrics, gynecology, surgery, medicine, pediatrics, etc. Studying was no longer a chore; it was my passion, a way of relaxing.

During the junior year, on each clinical rotation, medical students were scheduled to work until eleven o'clock in the evening. It was a real relief to find out that seniors, on their clinical rotations, spent the night in the hospital. Leaving either Children's Hospital or Louisville General Hospital after dark was a risky venture. I was able to get a job in the Louisville General Hospital Anesthesia Department for the summer between my junior and senior year. I continued to take night call in the anesthesia department during my senior year. The anesthesia call room was in the basement of the hospital, right next to the sidewalk that ran in front of the hospital. Many nights, we would hear people running and cursing, and then we would listen to the sounds of gunfire. When that happened, two of us would get up and head for the operating rooms. Usually, by the time we had IV fluids hanging, endotracheal tubes laid out, and the anesthesia machines ready, in would roll in one or two wounded people. Every time that happened, I was relieved that I had not been required to leave to go home that night.

Occasionally, patients arrived with gunshot wounds of the heart. Louisville General Hospital had the highest survival rate of any hospital when it comes to caring for those with gunshot wounds to the heart. The survival of those patients was largely due to the fact that the Louisville police had the authority to bypass the emergency room with the most seriously injured people and to send those straight to operating rooms.

When the calls came in, the operating room crew, anesthesia personnel, X-ray technicians with their equipment, and surgery residents would be waiting, ready to cut. Sometimes, immediate surgery was not needed, and, sometimes, we had the opportunity to talk with the patient. One of the most memorable conversations was with a young man from eastern Kentucky, who had been stabbed in the chest very close to the heart. I asked him, "Who stabbed you?"

In his unbelievably strong hillbilly accent, he replied, "My best friend."

Then I asked him, "Why did he stab you?"

"Oh, it was over some old girl."

I told him that his friend had almost killed him and asked him if he was going to talk to the police about filing charges.

His surprising reply was, "No, I could never do that to my best friend."

Before starting my senior year, I was commissioned as a first lieutenant in the Air Force and went to the AFROTC office on the U of L campus to be sworn in by Captain Grubbs. The NCO staff all waited outside the front door of the building, and, at exactly the same moment, they gave me my first salute. I knew they had conspired to make sure that they all were the first one to salute me; that was expected, since it was traditional to hand a ten-dollar bill to the person who gives an officer his first salute. It was a proud moment; after years of wishing and waiting, I was an officer in the United States Air Force. That commission and a steady income made it possible for me to get married. Jackie Ochs had just graduated as a medical technologist; the income from her job, along with my income, allowed us to live far more comfortably than most of my classmates.

In October 1963, my military ID card enabled me to sign up for an opportunity to hunt deer on Fort Knox. I was assigned a specific area of the post where I would be able to hunt on November 24, 1963. On November 22, 1963, five of us, who were on a psychiatry rotation, along with one of the Psychiatry Department faculty members, were watching a patient interview. Suddenly, the door opened, and we were told that we were to go home and that President Kennedy had been shot. I left, unable to imagine what that would mean.

Two days later, I went deer hunting. My assigned area had been burned over by a forest fire only a week before. After finding my area, I left the car about an hour before first light. After only a few steps, I stepped in a hole about four feet deep. The fire had completely burned out a large tree stump, leaving a deep hole. Recovering from my shock and knowing that I would never again leave my flashlight behind, I waited in the car until first light. I shot my first deer about two miles from the car. By the time I got back to the car, I was exhausted and went to sleep in the car. Ten deer were feeding around the car when I awakened, and, of course, most were larger than the one I had carried and dragged for more than two hours. I drove back to show my deer to my parents. Suddenly, Granny opened the door to tell us that the police were getting ready to move Lee Harvey Oswald and that we could see him on TV. Along with millions of others, we watched Jack Ruby shoot President Kennedy's murderer. Some things never leave our memory, and that was one of those.

Six months before graduation, Mom graduated with a master's degree in accounting. She had told me that she would never let me finish school ahead of her. She kept that promise when she walked away with a bachelor's degree six months ahead me and a master's degree six months before I had my MD. She never let me catch up with her academically; she graduated with highest honors, while I only graduated with high honors. It didn't matter; I left medical school as a member of AOA, the medical school honor society. I left carrying a big dose of pride and arrogance.

WPAFB AND MAC DILL AFB

Graduation allowed for two weeks of fishing and water skiing on the Ohio River and some time to relax with friends. The last week in June was spent packing and moving to Fairborn, Ohio, to begin a rotating internship at the Wright-Patterson Air Force Base Hospital.

Interns work under different rules today. We were on call every other night. That meant that we worked from early one morning until the next night. When we were on call, we were up most of the night. Interns started their day by six thirty in the morning and got off at night when everything was finished; if you were on call the previous night, there was often enough work to keep you there until nine o'clock in the evening or later. The duty hours for interns and residents are now limited to sixteen-hour shifts instead of the thirty-three hours we used to work. Now, they must have eight to ten hours off between shifts, with total work hours per week not exceeding eighty hours. We had ten interns, and there were six specialty rotations of two months each, which were to be covered. The solution to the problem of covering all of the services was to have the two interns on the first rotation cover both pediatrics and the emergency room. My first rotation was on pediatrics. Roger Schorlemer and I were the two lucky ones who had to cover two services at the same time.

The year at WPAFB as an intern was exhausting; no time was ever available for reading, and free time was only a dream. My wife almost never saw me; as soon as supper was finished, it was time to go to sleep. I can only think of two occasions when we went out to eat. We only had one car, and that car went to the hospital with me. In retrospect, I have to wonder, how did Jackie deal with that year of isolation?

Life was much better after the year of internship. I was assigned to MacDill Air Force Base in Tampa, Florida. We bought a second car and a house. There was a privacy fence that was six feet high around the back yard. The fence was nice, but there was something strange about it. At the corners, each wall of the fence had its own corner post, and there was a four-inch space between the corner posts. I asked my next-door neighbor about the spaces at the corner. He laughed and said, "You bought old crazy Joe's house." The neighbors had all decided to build matching six-foot-tall fences on their own property to screen off Joe's property. Since they had built the fences inside their property lines, there was a resulting gap at the corners. I wish that I had met the previous owner; he must have been something special.

The best thing about being in Tampa was the proximity to Tampa Bay and the Gulf of Mexico, so as soon as possible, a boat was purchased. It was not very big, fifteen feet long; while a forty horsepower motor doesn't sound very powerful, it was enough to pull two skiers and was enough for some great fishing. Every day that I was not on call at the hospital, I would rush home, hook up the boat, put it in the water, and head for the grass flats to fish. There were occasions when several couples would go to St. Petersburg beach for a day of fishing, water skiing, and relaxing on the beach.

The MacDill AFB Hospital executive officer (XO) had previously been the head of urology at Wright-Patterson AFB Hospital and knew that my main interest was Obstetrics and Gynecology. No sooner had I reported for duty and headed to the medical clinic than I got a call to report to the XO's office. When his secretary sent me in to see him, I was offered some coffee and asked what my ideal assignment would be. After talking about my options, he decided to have me spend my mornings in the medical clinic and the afternoons in the Obstetrics and Gynecology clinic. I would then be taking OB/GYN call every forth night and MOD (medical officer of the day) call about once every three weeks. I would also be the hospital's physician representative on the mobility team. Several times, the call came in for everyone on the mobility team to report to a building adjacent to a runway. The first time that happened, a master sergeant said to me, "Doctor, I will tell you everything you need to know. You are to stay here until I say you can leave or tell you to board the plane. The coffee is over in the corner, meals will be brought in, cots are along the wall, and that is all you need to know." We were never told anything more. Usually, something would show up in the news a week or two later about some crisis in the world that had been averted.

One of the JAG (Judge Advocate General) officers—a lawyer—talked about brewing beer. The idea seemed intriguing, so I found a place to buy all the needed ingredients. Someone supplied me with three cases of quart-sized beer bottles in heavy cardboard boxes. I had heard that adding rice would result in a premium beer, and, with all the ingredients gathered, the process began. It seemed that the mixture was bubbling more than one would expect from the recipes, but, not being too concerned, I didn't discard the mixture.

That week, Jackie and I had decided that we should go to church and located one fairly close. Sunday morning, we went to church, and that evening I bottled my home brew. One case was placed on a shelf in the carport storage room, and I took a second case full of my premium beer with me on my way in to the hospital. Those bottles were given to several friends, including the JAG officer. After work, I drove into the carport and was surprised by the strong smell of beer. The beer bottles had exploded, blowing the bottoms out of the quart bottles, and had shot the bottles up through the cardboard cases. When I reached up to lift the cardboard case off of a shelf, beer ran down my arm, soaking my uniform. As I was mopping up the beer and picking up glass, the preacher from the church we had visited the day before walked around the storage room to find me wet with beer. He apologized for interrupting me and left. My guess was he didn't think I would be a good addition to his congregation. The next day, my friends told me that the beer bottles had exploded in their cars. That made me less than popular.

One of the patients in the OB clinic had an unusual name. We began talking about her last name and found out that she was the wife of a college friend. When she was in labor, he talked about taking a month of leave and asked me to fly with him on his first day back at work. He was a pilot of an F-4C Phantom, two-seat fighter/bomber. In order to make the flight, it was necessary to go through the decompression chamber and to get checked out on the use of the ejection seat. The day before he was to return to work and the day before our flight, he was asked to come back in to fly a bombing run. One of the pilots was sick, so he went in. On that flight, a very low level training mission bombing run, the plane's wingtip clipped a tree. The crash killed both pilots. Once again, I wondered how I had missed flying with him on that day and why God had protected me but not two of our country's very best.

Shortly after spending a year at MacDill, I got a call from an airman in the base's assignments section. I had just delivered his baby one week earlier. His call was to ask me if I wanted a spot in the Fitzsimons Army Hospital Obstetrics and Gynecology residency program. By that time, I had been accepted at the University of South Carolina for an OB/GYN residency and would be starting as soon as my service obligation was completed. The next week, he called again to ask me if I wanted to accept a transfer to Udorn AFB in Thailand. I turned down the offer because I was having a great time in Tampa. What I did not know was that when the Air Force offered you a good assignment, whether you accepted the offer or not, you were going to be reassigned. Two more weeks passed, and, once again, he called. This time, it was obvious that he was shaken. His wife's doctor had just received orders and would be quartered at an Army Special Forces camp in South Vietnam to be part of the Air Force's 552nd Medical Services Flight (MSF). He thought that being sent to a remote Special Forces camp was a death sentence.

That day, we put our house on the market. The house sold in about one week, the second car sold, and I moved Jackie back to Louisville, Kentucky, where she would live with her parents during my year in Vietnam.

USSF CAMP DAVID WIDDER

The first leg of the trip to Vietnam was a flight from Louisville, Kentucky, to Chicago. The plane began its take-off roll, and about the time it was to lift off, the power was cut and the plane returned to the gate. It was announced that a luggage door light had come on and that we would soon be taxiing out to take off. The thought came to me that this might be a bad omen. It wasn't. The next leg of the flight was from Chicago to Reno. Across the aisle from me was Wilt Chamberlain. He had an aisle seat, which was a good thing, since his legs stuck out in the aisle so far; it looked like his feet might reach the cockpit. That evening was spent in Sacramento, California. A bus ride later, Travis Air Force Base was finally reached. Late in the evening, a big C-5A cargo plane, equipped with seats, lifted off to take us to Tan Son Nhut Air Force Base outside of Saigon, Vietnam.

We disembarked and, after presenting our orders, were given directions to a hooch, where we spent the next day. The hooch was a building built with a frame of two-by-fours covered with screen wire, a metal roof, and boards that angled out from the screen wire. The boards deflected the rain without interfering with any cooling breezes that might come along. For nearly a year, buildings like that one would be my home. That first night in the country trying to sleep was difficult; the hooch was about one hundred feet from the main runway where jet fighter-bomber aircraft were taking off about every five minutes.

Early the next morning, an army bus took several of us to an old hotel in Saigon, next to a MACV (Military Assistance Command in Vietnam) building. For the next four days, we listened to lectures about our mission and the fact that we were to be a part of President Lyndon Johnson's efforts to "win the hearts and minds of the countrymen." Not only were the lectures boring, the old hotel was also a miserable place and had almost no water pressure. The commode's tank filled so slowly that it could only be flushed two times each day. The sink delivered water at a slow drip. Those days taught me that it was possible to bathe with a cup of water.

The lectures emphasized nine rules:

1. Remember we are guests here: We make no demands and seek no special treatment.
2. Join with the people! Understand their life, use phrases from their language
3. Treat women with politeness and respect.
4. Make personal friends among the soldiers and common people.
5. Always give the Vietnamese the right of way.
6. Be alert to security and ready to react with your military skill.
7. Don't attract attention by loud, rude, or unusual behavior.
8. Avoid separating yourself from the people by a display of wealth or privilege.
9. Above all else, you are members of the US Military Forces on a difficult mission, responsible for all your

official and personal actions. Reflect honor upon yourself and the United States of America.

Across the street from the hotel were homes of a type that was typical of Saigon. Concrete walls surrounded the small yards and houses. The tops of the walls were covered with broken glass cemented in place; the glass would certainly have deterred anyone who thought of climbing those walls. The last day gave me a look at a culture different from that known by Americans. There was a wedding across the street. Everyone was dressed in their finest. The women were wearing their beautiful *ao dai* dresses. The *ao dai* is usually white and is a full-length straight dress with full-length sleeves. The dress is worn over pants and is split down one side. The children were dressed in their finest too; however, their finest was different from anything I had ever seen. The pants had a two-inch wide opening extending from the beginning of the buttocks around to the front, allowing the child to defecate or urinate freely.

The following morning, we returned to Tan Son Nhut Air Base and were issued our M-16 rifles, six fifteen-round magazines, a .38 caliber revolver, a holster, and about two hundred rounds of ammunition. We were split up and left for our various assignments. The single engine Army Otter airplane flew me to a small rural town, Hon Quan, An Loc District, Binh Long Province. Dr. Paul Gleason, wearing a red beret, greeted me when the plane touched down; Paul made a career of the Air Force and eventually reached the rank of brigadier general. He was happy to see me; seeing me meant that his year in Vietnam was almost up and that he would soon be going home. I was his replacement. He drove me around the town, past an eight-inch howitzer, past the small hospital, past the Vietnamese LLDB (Luc

Luong Dac Biet, their special forces) camp, and finally to the US Special Forces camp, Camp David Widder. As we were sightseeing, he told me, "By the time two weeks are over, you will be able to rewrite every textbook of tropical medicine." He was right.

Walking up to the gate, a Vietnamese LLDB guard offered me a giant beetle. I shook my head no, and he popped that two-inch wide live beetle in his mouth and ate it. It was obvious that I wasn't back home in the States. The two-minute tour of the camp showed me that inside of the concertina wire-topped wall were concrete walled rooms called bunkers. Each of the bunkers had an opening to the outside to serve as a gun port for those who would occupy the bunker during any attacks. The bunkers had sandbags along the walls and covering the roof. There was one larger bunker that served as the medical bunker. Inside the compound were the well, a mess hall, two large hooches for the enlisted men, the latrine building, and the officer's three-room hooches. At each of the corners of the compound were enclosed guard posts, and at the gate was a guard post. The guard posts were manned each night by LLDB guards. Outside of the walled compound, there was a house used by two United States Agency for International Development (USAID) nurses, a parking lot for our jeeps, a shed with two diesel-powered generators, and the clubhouse. The camp was too small to have separate enlisted NCO and officers clubs.

Following the brief tour, the doctor that I was replacing drove me to a hospital in Hon Quan, a hospital for civilians. He explained that our unit, 552nd Medical Services Flight, was one of President Johnson's MILPHAP (Military Public Health Assistance Program) teams under the command of USAID (United States Agency for International

Development). There were forty teams, one for each of South Vietnam's forty provinces. To make up the forty teams, there were seven Air Force teams, seven army teams, six navy teams, and twenty military teams from other free world countries. The teams were all made up of three physicians, one medical service corps administrative officer, and ten medical corpsmen. Teams were provided housing with different situations in each province. Binh Long province was the least populated province, and, in order to house the 552nd MSF, our unit was assigned to the Special Forces B team camp in the town of An Loc. Our job was to provide medical care to civilians throughout the province. The first team had nearly completed their year in Vietnam and would be leaving over the next few weeks as members of our team replaced them.

The hospital and clinic were different from anything I had seen. There was what I remember to be thirty- to forty-bed ward. The beds were metal with a thin woven bamboo mat as the only mattress. Each bed had several patients. Patient's families stayed with them and bedded down in the aisles, between the beds, and under the beds. About half of the patients were emaciated, pale, weak, lethargic, and children appeared to be nothing but skin stretched over a skeleton; they looked like the pictures of those in the Nazi concentration camps. Nearly all of the patients were hospitalized because of malaria. The children all had malaria and worms. The more common worm infections were hookworms, tapeworms, the eight- to ten-inch *Ascaris lumbricoides*, and *Strongyloides stercoralis*.

In a separate building, there was a large waiting room and a room with several desks where a corpsman or doctor could sit as he talked with and examined his patients. Another building had three rooms that would serve as the laboratory, the sterilizer room, and the operating room. Down the hill was a building with the province medical chief's office, and a building with a delivery room and a postpartum ward. Off by itself was a morgue.

There was no electricity, and most of the buildings had open screen doors or no doors at all. Since the laboratory had no electricity, the microscope light source was a mirror aimed at the sky. Without a centrifuge to spin tubes of blood to check the hematocrit the percentage of a volume of blood made up by the red blood cells, a string was tied to the top of a tube of blood, and the tube was spun around the technician's head for several minutes. The most commonly ordered laboratory studies were a hematocrit and a differential. The differential requires smearing a drop of blood, determining the number of white blood cells, staining the dried smear, and counting the different types of white blood cells to obtain a percentage of the different types. To make up for the lack of a counter, one hundred small rocks were placed in a glass petri dish, and one rock was removed and placed on a labeled square of sheet of paper each for white blood cell seen. When all of the rocks had been removed, those on each square were counted to obtain the number of neutrophils, bands, lymphocytes, etc. All of our corpsmen found ways to function without equipment that would be considered essential in the US.

Next, we drove to Quan Loi, a French-owned golf course and swimming pool. The golf course bordered a French rubber plantation. On the way, I asked about the piece of angle iron that was welded to the front bumper. That angle iron extended a little higher than the windshield, and its purpose was to cut any wire that might be stretched across the road. The VC (Viet Cong) had been known to use a tightly stretched wire placed at just the right height to hit those in the front seat in the neck, decapitating them. The angle iron had been universally attached to US jeeps and had saved a number of lives. The jeeps were driven without a top and doors and with the windshield down. That way, the windshield would not be an obstruction in the event it was necessary to begin firing over the hood. It would also be easy to jump out of the jeep in the event of an attack. The red berets worn by the members of the 552 MSF were chosen to allow the Vietnamese to differentiate our people from other US forces. It was explained that most of the enemy were Viet Cong and that they often came in civilian clothes seeking care and that about half of our patients were probably VC family members. As far as any VC attack was concerned, the 552 MSF was off-limits. With our red berets, we could go anywhere without any fear of attack; the only things we needed to fear were land mines, booby traps, and, possibly, an attack on our camp.

When we arrived at Quan Loi and began to look around at the golf course and the surrounding rubber trees, we heard the tinkle of a bell. The sound was coming from a three-wheeled bike. There were two wheels in front, and a metal box was mounted on the front. The rider was a girl, wearing an *ao dai* and a wide straw hat. The bell on the handlebars was used to get our attention. When she reached us, she lifted the top of the box and revealed about a case of soft drinks and ice. We each bought a Coca Cola and drank it, all the while thinking with amazement about the fact that out there, miles away from anyone, she had brought us some ice-cold cokes.

A few weeks later, Quan Loi ceased to be a beautiful place. Big Red One, the 1st Infantry Division, brought in a brigade to set up a base of operations. The pool and the golf course were bulldozed flat in order to build a runway made of laterite. Laterite is a form of soil that is very high in iron, which was used throughout South Vietnam as a surface for runways. The troops all dug holes about four feet by six feet and about four and one-half feet deep. Wood pallets were placed at the bottom of the hole. The pallets served as floor, and since the pallets were about five inches in thickness, that kept the men out of the water that would collect during the rainy season. A canvas cover provided shelter, and that was home for the men in the brigade.

A few days after my arrival, Dr. John Gartland and Dr. Jerry Jones arrived along with First Lieutenant John Porter, our administrative officer. Jerry had only recently been commissioned as a captain; John had been commissioned when he received a Berry Plan deferment to allow him to do an orthopedic surgery residency. When he decided to change his specialty to that of radiology, he lost his deferment and was called to active duty. The camp commander called us into his room and explained that since John had been commissioned as a captain a few days before I started my internship and was promoted to the rank of captain, John would be our unit commander based on the day of rank. That was great; John would have to stay in camp whenever the Special Forces or other army units called for a doctor, and being the next highest in rank gave me the option of being the one to go. I did go from that day on for the rest of my year in Vietnam.

THE CLINIC

Many of the patients made it easy for us to quickly diagnose their problems. As I mentioned earlier, when mothers brought in toddlers that were pale, emaciated, and listless, we immediately knew their diagnosis with one hundred percent certainty. On examination, they always had hepatomegaly (enlarged liver) and splenomegaly (enlarged spleen) due to malaria. Laboratory testing always confirmed our impression that they had anemia (low red blood cell count) from losing blood as a result of hookworms in the intestinal tract and from the breakdown of red blood cells caused by the malaria organisms. Nearly every time, a blood smear demonstrated the very deadly falciparum malaria organisms in the red blood cells. A stool specimen would be filled with hookworm eggs and often eggs of other parasitic worms.

The Plasmodium falciparum malaria organism in South Vietnam was resistant to the drugs, chloroquine, and primiquine but was sensitive to the easily available quinine. The problem we faced was that even though we could treat the malaria and the parasitic infestation, the patients were often too weak to survive without hospitalization. In the hospital, we could make certain that the children received their medications and a diet that would give them the protein, iron, and vitamins that their body required. To our dismay, after one day, the mothers would usually leave, and we were fairly certain that many of those children would die at home.

Adults with malaria could often be diagnosed before they ever even made it into the clinic. On arriving at the hospital in the morning, we would often see patients arriving with a towel wrapped around their head and with dark circles in the center of their forehead and over their chest. They would have linear dark bruise marks over the muscles of their arms. In the States, anyone with fever, headache, chest pain, coughing, and muscle aches would probably have the flu; in South Vietnam, they had malaria. The towel around the head told us that they had a fever. The circular bruises were from cupping. The Vietnamese would hold a cup or glass upside down and heat the air inside the cup or glass with a match or candle. The cup or glass was then placed over the forehead and over about six spots on the front and back of the chest. As the air in the cup cooled and contracted, it created a suction that resulted in rupturing of the capillaries of the skin. The small amount of bleeding in the skin caused pigmented circles to appear. The idea behind this process called *cupping* was to draw out the pain. The marks on the muscles of the arms and often on the legs were a result of rubbing the muscles as their witch doctors made an effort to rub away the pain. When all of that failed, the sick person would come to the clinic.

There were Vietnamese health worker students who saw patients with us and generally impressed us with their abilities. These students were to complete a two-year preceptorship prior to being sent out to work in small towns, where they would be the only source of health care for most of the people. They quickly learned techniques for suturing lacerations and learned to do dental extractions. As a medical student, I had spent a lot of time working in the anesthesia department; that time proved to be very valuable, as it gave me the background to teach students the techniques for performing regional blocks that they could use on dental patients who needed several teeth extracted. Anyone with a laceration or needing a tooth pulled was sent to one of the health worker students who did a great job. Most of the people in our area chewed sugarcane almost constantly and had terrible tooth decay with cavities and loose teeth.

Many of the Vietnamese had red saliva and drooled the spittle onto their cheeks and chin. The stained saliva was from chewing betel nut and betel leaves. Both have a mild narcotic effect and are apparently addictive. Those users end up with black teeth. When they lost all of their teeth, the only place they could get dentures was at jewelry stores. Most of the jewelry stores in Saigon had dentures in their display windows, where the buyer had a choice of dentures with either white or black teeth. I wish I had bought a set of the black teeth as a souvenir of Vietnam.

Just as was common in rural areas of the USA years ago, many people tried to treat localized pain with poultices, soft wet packs of some substance with a supposed medical benefit. In our area of Vietnam, water buffalo dung was most often the poultice. We quite often saw patients who had areas crusted with water buffalo dung in an effort to draw out pain. One child was brought in with a high fracture of the humerus (the bone in the upper arm). He was quite ill with a high fever, and his arm and shoulder were extremely swollen, tender, and very obviously infected. He was so ill that there was concern about whether he would survive. The entire area was crusted with water buffalo dung. His parents had packed the shoulder with dung, and then they had repeatedly punched a needle through the dung into the area of pain. It was surprising that antibiotics were effective in treating the ensuing infection. He left the hospital with his infection cured and a sling to help position the arm so that the fracture could heal.

Many of the patients were Montagnards, a primitive tribal people. They traveled on foot and would often arrive carrying a patient. On one occasion, we saw three Montagnard men walking from the Quan Loi airport area, heading toward our hospital, a distance of about four miles. Two were walking with a large bamboo pole riding on their shoulders. Suspended from the pole was a man wrapped in a blanket. He had become comatose after developing a fever, chills, and black urine (black water fever from malaria). To us, it was obvious that he was dying from cerebral malaria, and, in fact, he died as one of our corpsmen was checking him.

One of the Montagnard families brought in a child who had been bitten by a dog. It is customary in the States that if someone is bitten, the dog will be captured, and, if there is no evidence that the dog has been vaccinated for rabies, the dog will be quarantined for two weeks. If the dog remains healthy, then the dog bite victim does not have to go through the series of expensive and painful rabies vaccinations. The Montagnards rarely offered any information and would usually only answer questions with a single word. I had the interpreter ask, "When was he bitten?" After getting the answer, "Yesterday," I asked, "Was it your dog that bit him?" The father answered, "No." Then I asked, "Is the dog from your village?" The answer was, "No." The next question was, "Was the dog acting strange?" Again, there was a one-word answer, "Yes." Then I asked, "Can you catch the dog and bring it to us?" The answer was, "No." Then I asked why they could not catch the dog, and he answered, "We ate it." Needless to say, the child had to be immunized. I never could find out if a person can get rabies from eating a cooked dog.

Even though we all knew that many of our patients, including their families, were Viet Cong, we were still in for a surprise one morning. A male patient in his forties had been seen in the clinic by one of our corpsmen. Treatment was started, and he was instructed to return several times to make sure that he was responding well. He had only spoken Vietnamese on those visits; a translator had been required for each visit. On his last visit, after being told that he was doing well and would not need to be seen again, he expressed his thanks speaking in perfect Oxford English. He then told those in the clinic that he was a VC colonel, a battalion commander, and that he wished to turn himself in under the Chu Hoi safe passage program because he wanted to fight for our side. With that, he handed over his pistol. One of the Special Forces responded to our call and came to join him for a helicopter flight to a Chu Hoi retraining camp.

LANGUAGE CLASSES

From the first, it became apparent that we should make an attempt to learn the language and that we should help the hospital's staff with their English. I offered to work with the nurses. Since I knew that they were already fluent in English and really didn't need any one to teach them, that was really a selfish offer; I just wanted the easiest job.

The first minute of the first class gave me a shock; one of the midwives raised her hand and asked, "*Bac Si* 'Rober,' what is a gerund?" My early education was in a one-room school in Kentucky, could she really think I would know what a gerund was? I had learned enough to know that the best answer in a situation like that was to ask her a question. So I asked her what she thought a gerund was, and she told me. I knew she had studied English grammar all the way through school and was much more knowledgeable than I was, so I congratulated her on being right. It turned out that she really was right. I subscribed to *Time* and *US News & World Report* and had the nurses pass those around. Once a week, each of them was to read their favorite article and discuss it in English. Their conversational English quickly improved.

One of the Vietnamese interpreters was a college graduate, who was fluent in English, French, German, the Montagnard language, and, of course, his native Vietnamese.

John Gartland, John Porter, the two American nurses, and I asked him to teach us Vietnamese. We ordered some basic textbooks and began our lessons. For about nine months, we met in the house used by the two nurses and the two translators. Evenings with a cool breeze, a drink, and friends were the highlight of our week, as we tried to learn a new language. Vietnamese is a tonal language, and, as such, the same printed word may have several totally different meanings with a very slight tonal change. We all tried our best, but Vietnamese was very difficult to learn. After a while, we were able to ask basic questions and give basic instructions, such as, "Take a deep breath."

With a few basic phrases, we were able enjoy an occasional restaurant outing where we could practice our language skills. In the town of Hon Quan, there were two restaurants, a Vietnamese and a Chinese restaurant. Most of the time, we would order chicken dishes. The chicken was always cut up into pieces so that it could be eaten with chopsticks. When I say the chicken was cut up, I mean cut up. The cooks used a meat cleaver to cut the chicken into bite-size pieces, bones and all. I don't remember which was which, but, at one of the restaurants, the polite way of disposing of the bones was to spit the fragments onto a plate. In the other restaurant, the polite way was to spit the bone fragments onto the floor.

Occasionally, when two of us went to Saigon to pick up supplies, we would go to a restaurant named Cheap Charlie's. A couple of times, a few other military personnel joined us for supper. The Vietnamese restaurant staff was always surprised to have an American order in Vietnamese. They were even more surprised to have someone joke with them in their language. My favorite trick was to speak Vietnamese and go around the table ordering each man a cold beer and, finally, ordering a glass of warm urine for the last one of our group. The restaurant would explode in laughter. The waitresses would run into the kitchen and return with the cooks. They would all be shrieking and laughing while pointing at the one uncomprehending and embarrassed member of our group.

SUPPLY LINES

The hospital and clinic were under the Vietnam Ministry of Health, and our supplies were supposed to come through the ARVN (Army of the Republic of Vietnam) medical depot in Saigon. The problem was, no matter what was ordered, almost no supplies were ever issued. We could get quinine, a medication for malaria, medications for treating those infested with worms but almost nothing else.

During my first six months there, the only antibiotic issued was Bicillin. Bicillin is good for treating strep throat and syphilis but basically nothing else. However, those in the military services all know that there are three words that they live by: mission, mission, and mission. Officers formulate and direct the mission; non-commissioned officers (NCO's) do what it takes to carry out the mission, and our fighting men all know that you do whatever it takes. Our mission was to provide good health care to the people of Binh Long Province; to carry out our mission, our NCO's found ways to get the supplies we needed.

Our supply sergeant came to me with a proposal. He asked if I would talk with Dr. Gartland and the Special Forces camp commander to get permission to open a PX (post exchange on Army installations and base exchange on Air Force installations). He said that if we opened a PX, we could sell a good many cameras and other expensive items to not only the men in our camp but also to the many troops that passed through the area. He also talked about the fact that the PX could then take over the task of purchasing all soft drinks and alcoholic drinks for the camp. Then the secret to supplying the hospital was explained. The exchange system allowed each PX a breakage rate on everything it purchased. That meant that we would be allowed a ten-percent breakage on cameras and other items and up to twenty-percent breakage on liquor, and these "broken" items could be written off.

As the discussion progressed, he pointed out that with the exception of Dr. Gartland and Dr. Jones, we had all been on active duty at different air bases, and all of us knew hospital supply sergeants from our previous stations. Most of those supply sergeants had been reassigned and were stationed in Air Force bases all around Vietnam. In my case, I had been stationed at MacDill AFB in Florida. That was the home of the 15th Tactical Fighter Wing, which had been assigned to Cam Rahn Bay AFB on the coast of South Vietnam. I knew some of the nurses, fighter pilots, and the hospital supply NCOIC (non-commissioned officer in charge). I was then educated about the fact that with a "broken" Nikon camera, a "broken" case of Chivas Regal, a VC flag, and a Montagnard crossbow, the world of supplies would open to me. What we knew was that all military men want to help each other, and that supply sergeants would share anything that they had not personally signed for.

From that time on, supplies began to pour in. About once every two weeks, one or two of us would catch a flight to Saigon and then to a base where we had contacts with supply sergeants. I loaded up a duffel bag with crossbows and "broken" items and flew in to Cam Rahn Bay where I spent some time with the hospital supply sergeant, gave him my bagful of goodies, and enjoyed a couple of days of relaxation on the beach. If we had won the war, I believe that Cam Rahn Bay, with its beautiful beach, would now be a big tourist center. When I told the supply sergeant that I was ready to leave, I was directed to a C-130, a large cargo airplane. That plane was almost completely filled with medical supplies that had somehow appeared as if by magic. When I got to Saigon, those supplies were transferred to two Caribou aircraft. The Caribou was a two-engine cargo aircraft and was the largest airplane that could land on our airstrip. After transferring the supplies to the aircraft and unloading everything at our airstrip, it took several hours to move everything into the hospital.

Occasionally, we would receive unexpected boxes from UNICEF (United Nations Children's Fund). One UNICEF shipment brought us surgical caps and masks as well as enough gowns for a hospital much larger than ours and surgical drapes. Another shipment solved a big problem; we received hundreds of bottles of a German manufactured plasma expander IV fluid. We very seldom needed to give a volume expander, something usually given to patients in shock from blood loss. As always, nothing ever went to waste; our corpsmen found another use for the IV volume expander fluids. Our hospital didn't have running water, so we couldn't scrub up before we operated and were not even able to wash our hands and arms before putting on our gowns and gloves for surgery. The volume expander was sterile and was the answer to our problem of not having the water we needed to scrub up prior to entering the operating room. Before each case, someone would pour the fluid over our hands and arms as we did our surgical scrub.

The fluids were also used in scrubbing the patient before putting on the sterile surgical drapes.

Our most valued UNICEF shipment brought us a British anesthesia machine that was made to administer a general anesthesia using ether. That machine was made to be air-dropped to commandos and was an amazing piece of equipment. It was in a wooden case, and, when we took it out of the case, we saw that it had a bellows, which would allow patients to be ventilated, and on top of the larger metal portion a one-inch brass screw top that when opened revealed a brass vial for ether. There were tubes that could be connected to a facemask or endotracheal tube. That machine could administer a controlled anesthetic mixture of air and ether gas. Ether is no longer used in most developed countries for two reasons. The first reason is that for a long time, there was no way to control the level of anesthesia and patients would wake up with severe nausea and vomiting. The second reason ether is not used is that it is flammable. That machine delivered a controlled mixture of air and ether that eliminated the postoperative nausea. It opened up the possibility of developing a very active surgical service.

The machine was so very easy to use that I could teach our corpsmen and nurses to administer general anesthetics. That very fact provided an answer to a very perplexing problem. We were very aware that the war could not last forever and that an American medical team would not be there very long. It seemed unlikely that there would be a Vietnamese doctor to take over when we left. Many times when we needed to transport a patient to a major hospital, helicopters were not available, and ambulances could not safely traverse a war zone to make the eighty-mile trip to Saigon. We knew that without the capability of an emergency abdominal delivery (cesarean section), there would be mothers and babies who would die. With that in mind, the two Vietnamese nurse midwives were excited about the possibility that they could learn to give anesthesia and perform cesarean section deliveries. Then when they were faced with life and death emergencies, even without a physician or hospital referral available, they could manage the problems. The nurse midwives were well-educated and very capable; they learned quickly, and soon I was no longer acting as the surgeon but became the first assistant on cesarean section deliveries as one nurse midwife gave anesthesia and the other operated.

Five days of each week, the mail plane would come in at about four o'clock in the afternoon. That plane was a two-engine Caribou that made its rounds of several Special Forces camp airstrips dropping off supplies and mail. Our clinic would usually be winding down by the time the mail plane appeared, so we told the Special Forces NCOIC that we would take care of meeting the mail plane.

One day, 1st Lt. John Porter drove to the airstrip to get the mail. When the plane landed, one of the crew said, "You must be the refugee rep." John answered, "What?" He was handed a piece of paper and was told to sign it. At that same time, the crew on the plane off-loaded a stack of metal beams and sheet metal roofing and flew away. John called for us to bring some men and a truck to pick up what must have been part of a prefabricated building. As I mentioned earlier, NCOs make the military what it is. I never even knew how the 1st Infantry Division people found out about the building, but, a few days later, we were covered up with men and equipment. They brought a large generator; up to that time, there were days when we had not had any electricity. In two or three days, the concrete floor was poured, the frame was erected, and the building had been roofed. A well was drilled, and with electricity a pump was in, and running water became a possibility. Those troops from Big Red One probably never realized how much their volunteered efforts helped improve the lives of the Vietnamese people. We really did appreciate their help, and it still amazes me when I think of how much those men enjoyed helping us and never expected anyone to say thanks.

That building was to have an operating room and X-ray room. Prisoners from the local jail always vied to see who could come work at the hospital. They could get out of jail for a day, get snacks and cigarettes, and enjoy doing something worthwhile. Soon, they were hard at work making bricks and walling up the building.

John Porter told me that he had gone over the requisitions and found that the previous team had repeatedly requisitioned an X-ray unit. He thought he knew how to get that order filled, whether the Vietnamese wanted to fill it or not. The next day, the two of us flew in to Ton Son Nhut for what would be my final supply trip. We went in to Saigon, where we spent the night, and went to the top of the Rex Hotel for a drink before calling it a night. While we sat there in comfort, the war was going on a short distance away on the Saigon River. It seemed unreal that we could sit there in comfort and watch helicopter gunships exchanging fire with the VC, knowing that men were being killed while we relaxed and cheered for our team.

The next morning, I got up early and went for a walk. Along the way, I noticed a brown leather folder lying in the gutter. It contained a very official-looking document signed by Her Majesty, the Queen of England. I took it to the American Embassy and handed it to a marine sergeant. He asked me to have a seat and informed me that I was not to leave until he gave me permission. After about thirty minutes, he returned and said, "Sir, you may now leave." To this day, how that document ended up in a gutter in Saigon is still a mystery.

John and I joined up and went to Ton Son Nhut AFB, signed out a truck, and drove to the ARVN medical depot. John told me to go in, raise sand, and get everyone tied up trying to figure out why we had never gotten an X-ray machine. Then he told me that when he showed up, I was to leave immediately and get in the truck, as we would be leaving quickly. While I was in the office creating a ruckus, he went out into the depot and found a crated X-ray unit. When he did, he used a black marker pen to write "Binh Long Hospital" on the wooden crate. Then he found a worker with a forklift, had the man follow him and load the crate on our truck. When I saw John, I told everyone, "Thanks for trying to help me." We quickly drove away with our new X-ray unit and loaded it into the mail plane. Soon, electricians from Big Red One showed up. In just a few days, we had a working X-ray unit and a fully working operating room with a real operating room light.

On one supply run, while sitting comfortably in an airplane that was flying along at about 3,500 feet, there was a loud crack. About an inch from my right foot, there was a nice round bullet hole and another above my head. Obviously, a bullet had hit close to me, but I escaped unharmed. When I tell people about that, I am usually asked, "What did you do then?" My answer is, there was nothing I could do. Once again, I have to think that God had protected me, and I often wonder why.

SURGERY

At the time I arrived, surgical capabilities were very limited. The hospital had some vials of local anesthetics and a few vials that could be used for a spinal anesthetic. We did have an ancient metal operating table in one room in the clinic area. That room had a screen door on both the front and back. John Gartland had finished one year of general surgery and part of an orthopedic surgery residency. I had a year of experience in obstetrics and gynecology, as well as having spent over a year giving anesthesia. We decided that we could develop an active surgery service. Prior to our arrival, the closest places that offered surgical care to Vietnamese were the Cholon Hospital in Saigon and the German hospital ship, the *Helgoland*, which was docked in Saigon. Interestingly, forty-five years after I left Vietnam, every Wednesday morning, I began meeting with a Vietnam War medevac pilot and his wife at the Regis Café in Red Lodge, Montana, for a breakfast Bible study. She was originally from Germany and had been a nurse on the German Red Cross hospital ship, the *Helgoland*. We had probably met when I toured the ship on one of my trips to Saigon.

It was important to develop a surgical service, since getting Vietnamese patients through a war zone for surgery was a real problem. We began small, using what equipment we had and doing those operations that could be performed with a local anesthetic. As supplies came in, we progressed to the point of doing major operations using spinal anesthesia.

It is amazing to look back at pictures of some of our earliest surgical cases. We didn't have gowns or masks and caps for everyone. Surgery quickly became Hon Quan's biggest attraction. Kids would gather outside of the operating rooms and look in through the open back door; sometimes, they even came in to watch the show. One of our corpsmen came up with some two-by-four lumber and made a stand, much like a standing coat rack to which he attached a jeep headlight; who knows where he found that headlight? From the light, he ran a set of jumper cables out the front door of the OR, lifted up the seat of a jeep to expose the battery, and clipped the cables to the battery. For most of the year, a jeep headlight was our operating room light. In a few weeks, we had a metal stand for the light.

Maintaining a sterile operating room was not easy. When a cow stuck her head through the door to watch us, it was time to make some changes. Once again, things just seemed to come from nowhere; our corpsmen certainly had contacts. A few days after the episode with the cow, fence posts, posthole diggers, barbed wire, and prisoners appeared. After they had set the posts, the prisoners began to put up the wire, pulling it by hand in an effort to draw the wire tight. I stopped what I was doing and went out to help them and showed them that the wire could be stretched with a clawhammer, and a second hammer could be used to staple wire to the posts. Two of the Vietnamese nurses ran out to tell me, "*Bac Si*, you work with your mind. It is not proper for you to work with your hands." It was the first time I ever knew that.

After the UNICEF shipment with the ether machine arrived, we began to operate on a regular basis. One memorable case was that of a lady who came to the clinic complaining that she had been pregnant for two years, and she certainly looked the part. She had a large, benign mucinous cystadenoma of the ovary that weighed twenty-eight pounds. She left in a few days, thankful and looking very different. As word began to spread, more and more people came, wanting to have surgery. It was not long before women began bringing in their children for hernia repairs. Soon, John was busy spending a lot of his time repairing hernias. Some other, and often unusual, cases came in. One day, he operated on a barber who had a lipoma, a fatty tumor, the size of a large grapefruit. About two weeks later, the barber returned, bringing his friend who also had a lipoma the size of a large grapefruit.

Right before my year in Vietnam ended, the X-ray and surgical building were completed. I have always regretted that I didn't get to use the new operating room before I left.

NURSE MIDWIVES

The two nurse midwives were well-educated, very capable, and beautiful. Fortunately, I was married and was looking forward to the day I could go back home to my wife. Our two single doctors and a number of single corpsmen might have been interested in rotating back to the States with one of them as their wife had it not been for two things. First of all, our Special Forces camp commander regularly reminded everyone that we were absolutely not to develop close relationships with any Vietnamese woman; if we did, he promised to push for a court martial on the basis of disobeying his orders. He emphasized that the Special Forces and also our unit could only function if we were diligent to maintain good relationships with the local people. If we became involved with the local women, it would not be long before resentment and anger would build among the Vietnamese. The second thing was that the US government made it impossible for a member of the armed forces to marry one of the Vietnamese women and take that wife back to the US. That didn't keep our men from looking.

While a metal instrument, known as the vacuum extractor, was described in all of the obstetrics textbooks, I had never seen one used and had never met anyone who knew how to use one. The device had a cup that was applied to the head of the baby as it descended through the birth canal. Suction was created by the use of a pump, producing a seal that attached the cup to the baby's head. Traction was applied to help the baby come through the birth canal. Using it, the midwives were able to deliver babies that otherwise could have only been delivered by the use of forceps or by cesarean section. They were quite surprised that I didn't know how to use a vacuum extractor and began calling me whenever there was a patient whose labor was not progressing well. With their help, I soon became proficient in its use. Later on in my obstetrics and gynecology residency, there were opportunities to pass that knowledge on to younger residents. A few years later, vacuum extractors that used a soft plastic cup were developed and came into common use in the States.

Before my assignment to Vietnam, I had been accepted into the four-year obstetrics and gynecology residency program at the Medical College of South Carolina in Charleston, South Carolina. I was to start there as soon as my military service obligation was over. Knowing that I would be in Charleston for my residency, I had asked that my next assignment would be at Charleston AFB for my last year in the Air Force. The OB/GYN residents in Charleston asked me to join them for their monthly journal club meeting. That meeting was held at a restaurant, and, after a meal, three of the residents would each present an article from a medical journal. They asked Dr. Lawrence Hester, the chairman of the residency program, if I could take the program one night and talk about my experiences in Vietnam. As a part of my talk, I talked about the nurse midwives and showed slides of them giving anesthesia and performing cesarean section deliveries.

As we were leaving, several of the residents came up to me and told me that they should have warned me that Dr.

Hester and all of the faculty did not like midwives and that Dr. Hester was pushing the state legislature to put a stop to midwives delivering babies. Those residents expressed the fear that because of my talk, I might have lost my opportunity to do my residency there in Charleston. I later found out that South Carolina had a number of "Granny Midwives," untrained women who lived in small rural towns and stood by for deliveries, often with bad results and with some maternal deaths. In fact, at that time, there was only one nurse midwife program in the United States, and it was a non-university program in Eastern Kentucky. That program trained nurse midwives who would serve in remote Appalachian Mountain communities.

At the end of my second year of residency, Dr. Hester announced that he was taking a year of sabbatical leave and that he would be working in a hospital in England. When he returned, he called me into his office. Being called into Dr. Hester's office was always frightening. I sat outside his office for about an hour, wondering what I had done wrong. When I finally went in, he asked me to have a seat and then to my great relief, he told me that his reason for going to England was to study their nurse midwifery training programs; he had been very intrigued with my remarks about the nurse midwives in Vietnam. Then he told me that in a year, his department would be the first in the United States to begin a training program for nurse midwives. There are now a number of such programs all over the United States training nurse midwives who provide excellent care. Looking back, I am amazed that I was able to play even a tiny role in getting that profession going in the states. Two wonderful ladies in Vietnam will never know of the positive impact that they had on the health care of women; they really deserve a round of applause.

DR. JONES

The most interesting person I have ever known is Dr. Jerry Jones. He arrived and got the tour of the area and the hospital. That first night, he seemed very quiet. The next morning, Jerry made hospital rounds with us and went to the clinic. At around ten o'clock that morning, I was busy managing several patients who had minor lacerations and helping the Vietnamese health worker students with their suturing techniques. About halfway through the morning, one of the corpsmen came looking for me and asked if I could help out in the clinic. On the way to the clinic, I asked if Dr. Jones was there. The corpsman told me that Dr. Jones had suddenly left and, on the way out, had said, "I'm never doing this again."

For the next two weeks, Jerry never put on his uniform fatigues; instead, he wore plaid or stripped shirts and plaid or striped shorts and tennis shoes. He only got out of bed to eat or to go to the shower and latrine. By the end of two weeks, some of the Special Forces men were coming to me to ask me what we were going to do with Dr. Jones. The next thing that I knew was that he began typing, sitting in his room and working at his typewriter from early in the morning until late at night. That went on for weeks. He never said a word about what he was doing. He only came out of his room to eat, but he did pull guard duty

Dr. David Roberts

in uniform and not in his usual stripped or plaid shirts and shorts.

One morning, the Vietnamese nurses came to me to tell me that they had seen Dr. Jones. I was told that he was wearing his uniform and that he had a notebook with him. They said that he had gone into the Province Health Director's office. About an hour or two later, he came out, and we watched as the health director and Jerry bowed to each other several times. After that, he got into a jeep and left. In time, we found out that Jerry had been very distressed, and even depressed, by what he had seen in the hospital and in the clinic. While he had been lying in bed those two weeks, he had formulated a three-step public health plan that would save hundreds and probably thousands of lives. When he had gone in to see the province health director, he had presented the completed plan. From there, he had gone to the province chief's office and to the Special Forces commanding officer to present his plan.

What he knew and what we had not considered was that most of the illnesses and deaths in our area of Vietnam were unnecessary and preventable. He knew that in South Vietnam, most of the deaths from malaria, the many cases of severe malnutrition and worm infestation that had killed so many children, and the cholera outbreaks that would suddenly kill off half of the people in smaller villages could all be prevented by several simple measures.

Jerry knew that in South Vietnam the mosquitoes that carried malaria were house dwellers and lived on the ceilings during the day. At night, they flew down to bite humans. He also knew that the children and most of the adults defecated on the ground. When that happened, the eggs of the parasitic intestinal worms hatched in the soil, and then later larvae entered the bodies of children and adults by burrowing through the skin of their bare feet. The cholera epidemics were the result of asymptomatic carriers defecating on the ground and the bacteria washing into the streams. In most of the small villages, the only water source was found in streams next to the villages. When the rains washed the cholera organisms into the streams, there would be sudden outbreaks. Several times, we got an emergency call to tell us that a patrol had entered a village where there had been an outbreak of cholera and that a doctor was needed. One of the corpsmen and I would load up medical supplies and fly by helicopter to the village. Every time that happened, we found that about half of the people were dead and that the others were completely unaffected. On those occasions, there was nothing that could be done.

Jerry's plan was really quite simple. US forces were already carrying out MEDCAP (Medical Civic Action Program) operations. Units would go into towns and villages to help the people with any medical problems that could be handled on the spot. For the 552nd Medical Service Flight, that usually meant treating people for presumptive malaria infections, hookworms, other parasitic worms, and skin infections and helping them by extracting bad teeth.

The proposed plan meant that we would be involved in many MEDCAPs. The plan was for us to go into every village in Binh Long province. A few days before we were to go, Special Forces units or detachments from the 1st Infantry Division, and Vietnamese Army units were to enter the villages, where they would dig wells and cap those wells with concrete. Those capped wells would provide a clean water supply, which would prevent outbreaks of cholera and typhoid. Pit latrines would be built, eliminating the need for people to defecate on the ground. Those latrines would drastically reduce the many problems associated with parasitic infestations. Then a few days later, a two-man army spray team would accompany us for a MEDCAP mission in the villages that had the new wells and latrines. By the time that we were ready to put the plan into action, church groups from the US had sent clothing items for children and some of the women. UNICEF and other organizations had sent planeloads of rice in fifty-pound bags to be distributed among the villagers.

Once started, a convoy of military vehicles, our team, and enough troops to meet the security needs outlined by the Special Forces or First Infantry commanders would enter a town or village. The people were instructed to form a line; the very first step was to bathe the children. Next, using gas-powered injection guns, everyone was given typhoid and cholera vaccines. The Vietnamese children accepted the gas-powered injection guns much better than injections with a syringe and needle. After receiving their immunizations, medical and dental needs were addressed. When they reached the end of the line, adults were given rice and the children were given clothes, toothbrushes, and bars of soap. While the MEDCAP operation was in progress, a spray team entered each home, and, using DDT, an insecticide that is now banned, an "X" was sprayed on the ceilings to kill mosquitoes. The intent of those public health activities was to prevent most of the diseases we were seeing. The Special Forces liked participating in these activities because it gave them a chance to develop positive relationships with the people, and it gave them a chance to gather information about the level of VC activity in those villages.

In the process of carrying out the plan that Dr. Jones had developed, we worked out of each of the three A camps that were under the command of the B team, which made up Camp David Widder. I always enjoyed the nights spent at each of those A camps. While I was at the A camps, the Special Forces men let me join them firing mortars at random locations and, at random times, in what was known as harassment and interdiction fire.

The question is, how effective were the public health ventures? That question can be best answered by looking at the effect on the Hon Quan hospital and clinic. When we arrived in September and October, it was the height of the malaria season, each bed had several patients, and, sometimes, there were as many as four or five patients in and around a bed. Every day, there were adults and children who were dying from malnutrition and malaria. The clinic was crowded with patients who were suffering from malaria and parasitic diseases. By the next September, there was only one patient to a bed, and we often had empty beds. By then, malaria and parasitic diseases were uncommon.

About thirty years later, my brother-in-law, who was a navy captain, was looking around my office and spotted a framed certificate—The Air Force Outstanding Unit Award—that had been presented to the 552nd MSF. I had never thought anything about that award and had assumed that it was nothing more than the equivalent of a good conduct award. Bernie looked at it and expressed his amazement. That's when I found out that The Air Force Outstanding Unit Award was a big deal and that it was an award that was rarely given. We had earned that recognition not because of the work all of us in our unit had done in providing good medical care, but the award was primarily the result of Dr. Jones's work in the field of public health.

Dr. Jones was not through making life better for people. One morning, he was in the mess hall and suggested ways that the food could be improved. One of the Special Forces sergeants had been assigned to supervise the Vietnamese cook. When Dr. Jones shared his thoughts, the SF sergeant took offense and allowed as how Dr. Jones could take over. Jerry thanked him and took charge of the mess hall. I imagine that ours was the only army mess hall anywhere in the world that was run by an Air Force doctor. Suddenly, gourmet meals became routine. Jerry quickly found out that most American men were fans of the basic meat and potatoes fare, but, one day a week, we were treated to meals that were more imaginative than those served in most four- and five-star restaurants. Imagine being served flaming crepe suzettes in a mess hall.

The US military makes certain that our servicemen and women get good meals and considers that to be important in maintaining morale. Normally, food rations are delivered to units, but, during the Vietnam War, those in small units like the Special Forces camps and our unit were paid a per diem of thirty dollars each month, and we were to purchase food on the local economy. To deal with this, the Hon Quan Mess Association was formed. All of us were assessed a fee of thirty dollars each month. Larger units, such as the 1st Infantry Division brigade at Quan Loi, received large shipments of food. They always had more than they needed, since there were always men out on patrol, and the men in those units were issued C-Rations. With large units out on patrol, there was always an excess of rations. The brigade had to dispose of any extra food. Military forces were not allowed to give the extra rations to the Vietnamese, as much of it might end up in the hands of the enemy. They were required to dispose of the extra food by digging pits, pouring diesel fuel on the food, and then burying it. As you can imagine, no one liked the idea of destroying good steaks, shrimp, and other food items, and they were anxious to give it to our camp. Not needing to purchase food, the Hon Quan Mess Association money was used to purchase icemakers, refrigerators, and freezers. We gladly received Big Red One's extra rations, particularly the steaks, pork chops, shrimp, and other delicacies. Several days each week, Jerry would drive down to the center of Hon Quan to shop in the marketplace for fruits and vegetables to help round out our meals. I can say without any fear of being contradicted that the finest meals in the entire country were served at Camp David Widder.

Jerry's public health plan inspired me to try my hand at writing. For a number of months, I spent time at Jerry's typewriter, writing a handbook for Vietnamese rural health workers. In that handbook, I outlined most of the medical problems that they would encounter and the treatment for those conditions. Public health measures such as those formulated by Jerry were also included. Eventually, the handbook was translated, published, and distributed to rural health workers. Maybe that effort was helpful.

There can be no doubt that Dr. Jerry Jones, USAF captain, was the most interesting person I have ever met, and no one can overstate the importance of his contributions to the health and well-being of the people of Vietnam. I am thankful to have known him. His example has frequently been mentioned in my lectures to medical students and residents in some of the classes that I taught at Beacon University in Columbus, Georgia, at Yellowstone Baptist College in Billings, Montana, and at the Rocky Mountain College PA Program in Billings, Montana.

MEDCAPS

The Medical Civic Action Program instituted throughout South Vietnam not only involved MILPHAP (Military Public Health Assistance Program) teams but also involved many of our country's combat forces. Units would enter villages and provide as much medical care as possible during a period of one or two hours. When we entered the villages, the people were hesitant at first. Usually, that hesitance was based on the realization that the Viet Cong were known to come in shortly after the Americans left. From time to time, we would get reports that the VC had come in behind us, lined up the village officials, and killed them to punish everyone for having associated with the Americans.

When those in the 552nd MSF were involved in MEDCAP operations, we usually worked out of the small Special Forces A camps. A Special Forces A team was made up of around twelve men, who, along with varying numbers of Vietnamese troops, manned those camps. Those A camps were located in remote areas and were intended to block many of the enemy's movements and to control those remote areas. The Vietnamese troops that were associated with the US Special Forces were often not a part of the Republic of Vietnam Army but were men recruited, trained, and paid by the Special Forces. Those men could be classified as mercenaries.

Every trip was different. Several times, we worked out of Camp Widder. On those occasions, we were able to take a bigger team, since we would not be staying overnight at one of the smaller camps. One or two of our team, a couple of the health worker students, and occasionally one or both of our American nurses would be involved. On one of those trips, we went to a very scenic Montagnard village. The houses were one-room structures made of woven bamboo and elevated about eight feet above the ground. Each home had a woven bamboo fence around it. I started to walk down a path, planning to get some pictures, when I was grabbed from behind by one of the Special Forces sergeants. He spun me around and said, "Doc, don't you ever take another step, unless I am in front of you. This is a VC village, and there are going to be booby traps and mines. I get paid to know what to look for. You don't. If you wander off and get killed, I'll be blamed. Understand?" Those men will always be my heroes; they not only tolerated us, but they were also there for us, and we knew it.

There were three A camps under the control of the Special Forces B camp at Camp Widder. One of the three A camps we worked from was Minh Thanh, south of Hon Quan. That camp had a moat around it. Most of the time, the moat was dry, and, during the dry season, punji sticks were visible. Punji sticks were sharpened pieces of bamboo that had been stuck deep into the ground and which protruded about eight inches out of the soil. The VC also commonly used these as booby traps. In the event of an attack, the VC would have to cross a concertina wire barrier about ten feet wide, face a blast of steel balls from claymore mines, jump into the six-foot deep moat full of punji sticks, climb out of the moat, cross through another barrier of concertina wire, and then face rifle and machine gun fire, and probably fire from flame throwers. During my year in Vietnam, Minh Thanh was never attacked.

When I flew in to the Minh Than Special Forces camp to plan a MEDCAP, I got out of the helicopter; it lifted off, and its prop blast covered me in dirt. About an hour later, I learned just how fast I could take a shower. The shower facility consisted of a showerhead beneath an elevated platform, and on the platform was a steel drum full of water. During the day, the sun heated the water, so I was looking forward to a warm shower. The only problem was that it was late in the evening, the night was cold, and my chance to shower off came at about ten o'clock in the evening. Standing in the shower with a cold wind blowing and what felt like ice water pouring over me was a shock, not a treat.

The next day, a flatbed truck pulled up to the camp. The local Vietnamese officials wanted to make the MEDCAP a political and social event. We were promised security forces from ARVN and soon headed out for the nearest village. The flatbed truck had two large loudspeakers, and, while I sat on a stool situated on the bed of the truck, several Vietnamese stood around me, throwing out pamphlets and candy to all the children we passed. Only a short distance from the camp, we drove into a rubber tree plantation. Just as we got there, a large unit of US troops, which I think were from the 101st Airborne, pulled up in armored personnel carriers, and others off-loaded from helicopters. They immediately began to dig in, establishing a defensive position. You cannot imagine the looks we got from them as our truck with about five Vietnamese girls. Some men were throwing out pamphlets, and an Air Force doctor with a red beret came riding through with loudspeakers blaring out Vietnamese songs. I would have loved to hear the conversations that followed.

Several of the MEDCAP operations had us working out of the camp at Loch Ninh. Those MEDCAPS were primarily set up in the nearby town of Loch Ninh. We were told that the VC had recently come into town and had rounded up and killed several of the men as a show of force.

Each camp was very different. The Special Forces camp at Loch Ninh was to become the scene of a very large battle that took place shortly after I returned to the States. It was eventually overrun by the enemy, and I was later told that one of our 552nd MSF men was among those killed that day. That battle was so intense that over three thousand of the enemy were killed. At the time that I was in Vietnam, things were relatively quiet. I will try to describe the camp at Loch Ninh and some of the events that happened during my stay there.

The camp was located next to an airstrip. The outside bunkers were joined together to form a somewhat flattened four-pointed star and with gun ports facing out. The star shape allowed for overlapping fields of fire. Outside of the bunkers was the usual concertina wire and claymore mines that could be fired. The machine guns in those bunkers were on stands mounted in concrete, and the guns had chains attached that would prevent the machine guns being turned inward to fire on the camp. Inside of the bunkers were buildings that were built into the ground, with only about two feet of the walls being above ground. Those buildings were joined together to form a circle. Each building had small windows above ground level. Along the outside walls were benches that you could stand on in order to fire out of the windows in the event that the enemy made it past the bunkers. There were a few other buildings in the compound. At night, mortars were fired at random times and at random locations to harass the enemy.

On one of our trips to Loch Ninh, I was told that there were no extra beds and that the only place I could sleep in was on a folding canvas medical stretcher in a storage room. That seemed sufficient, so I made plans for the night. There was no mosquito netting, and it was a really hot night. I stripped down to my undershorts and tried to go to sleep. After a couple of hours of swatting mosquitoes, sleep finally came. What I did not know was that the local rat run was along a stack of boxes, and then the rats would jump down to the stretcher and, from there, onto the floor. About midnight, a rat jumped down, landed on my belly, and ran down my leg. I couldn't help it. I screamed. With that, everyone ran to their bunkers and began firing automatic weapons, covering every square inch of the perimeter. Someone began firing mortar flares, and, as I stood there in bewilderment, the door flew open, and I was face-to-face with a tough-looking Special Forces sergeant with his M-16 pointed at me.

He asked, "Was that you who screamed?" I admitted that I was the culprit and told him what had happened. After letting out a few good words, he said, "It'll take half the night to get everyone to stop shooting and get back to bed."

One morning, after we had spent a day working in the town of Loch Ninh, I was to fly out. When I went to get breakfast, the SF men were all scrambling around. When someone stopped long enough to talk to me, he told me to get my camera. Of all times, I had not brought it with me. Then he explained that shortly before breakfast, a member of an enemy, Khmer Rouge Battalion Headquarters Company, had come to the gate to arrange for the surrender of the company, along with the battalion commander and staff under the Chieu Hoi (Open Arms) Program.

During the war, the North Vietnamese, the Viet Cong, and Khmer Rouge communists had formed an alliance to fight US-backed forces. I was told that the Khmer Rouge, commonly called the KKK, wanted a large area of Cambodia and Vietnam and really didn't care who they fought as long as they could establish their own area of control. The planned surrender under the Chieu Hoi program would allow the Khmer Rouge unit to join with the army of Vietnam and the US army to fight for control of the area around Loch Ninh.

After breakfast, we all formed up and stood at attention inside the compound gate. The gate was opened, and an armed enemy company came marching in with their flag flying. The commander ordered them to halt, do a right face, and then had them stand at attention. He stepped forward, saluted, and handed over his pistol. Then he had his men step forward and stack their arms. After that, they were dismissed and as I remember, were fed breakfast. A short while later, planes landed and took the commander along with his men to Saigon to be retrained and returned to battle. I must admit, I was really uneasy for a few moments standing there as an armed enemy company marched into camp.

The Special Forces A camp, Tong Le Chon, was in a very remote area close to the Cambodian border. That camp was never used as a base of operation for any of our MEDCAP operations. I did get to that camp on three occasions and will devote the next chapter to memories of time spent there.

REPORTED DEAD

I only went to Camp Tong Le Chon three times. It was the most inhospitable place that anyone could imagine. Among Vietnamese people, it was known as "Tong Le Chon, numba ten," meaning that on a scale of one to ten, no place could be worse. The camp was situated on a hill close to the Cambodian border. It had been built using bulldozers to make up an eight to ten feet high circular dirt berm that was about twenty feet thick at the base.

In the berm were metal containerized freight boxes (conex boxes). The boxes had gun ports cut out on the outside, and the boxes were covered with sandbags. The conex boxes served as living quarters. Outside of the berm was the usual rolled concertina wire that made up the perimeter, and, of course, inside that perimeter were claymore mines. The camp was inside a VC controlled area and was the target of many attacks. Down the hill from the camp were a small lake and an airstrip suitable for aircraft as large as a C-130.

The first time I traveled to Tong Le Chon was at the invitation of one of the Special Forces officers. The camp's personnel had been caught up in a disagreement that had nearly progressed to the point of becoming a revolt. When we arrived there, it was obvious that even though calm had prevailed, things were still quite tense. That camp, like all of the Special Forces A camps, was manned by a Special Forces unit of about twelve men and a larger number of Vietnamese troops. On this occasion, the argument had started when the Vietnamese refused to go out on patrol and were refusing to carry out any of their duties. The basis for the disagreement almost seemed comical to an outsider.

That camp did not have a mess hall, and there was no kitchen. In most of the SF camps, meals were really quite good. At Tong Le Chon, everyone lived on C-Rations or what were called indigenous rations, which were dehydrated meals of rice along with dehydrated vegetables and meat. The Vietnamese had complained that they were being forced to eat rations that they didn't like. In an effort to please the Vietnamese, the camp commander had succeeded in getting a shipment of cattle and vegetables so that the Vietnamese troops could butcher the cattle and cook themselves some good meals with fresh vegetables and meat. After having had a great supper—a feast, really—the Vietnamese complained that they were too tired to go on patrol or perform any of their duties. Their reasoning was that they were too tired because they had to work to fix their meal while the Americans only had to open their C-Rations. Their refusal had almost become an armed conflict.

As things began to settle, I saw about ten Vietnamese troops walking out of the camp, laughing, carrying bamboo baskets, and wearing belts loaded down with grenades. When I asked about them, I was told that they were going fishing. Their method of fishing was to throw grenades into the lake and collect fish as they floated to the top.

My second trip to that camp was to take part in a special meal for all of the men in the camp. Men from the 1st Infantry brought in a field kitchen setup and served a great meal to everyone. That was a real morale booster for everybody.

The next trip was a far more somber event and was brought on by a battle that resulted in the death of one of the Special Forces sergeants from our camp. We got a request for a doctor. A patrol had come under attack, and the word was that reinforcements would be going in. As soon as I could grab two big duffel bags filled with supplies, a helicopter picked me up, and we headed for Tong Le Chon. It was a dark and overcast day with a light rain. After landing, I was told to be ready for casualties. A few minutes later, C-121 and C-130 aircraft began to arrive and dropped off a battalion-size unit of Vietnamese troops and their American advisers. I was told that the Vietnamese were Hmong tribesmen. As the hours passed, helicopters began bringing in dead Vietnamese troops. There were so many that they were stacked on wooden pallets so that a forklift could be used to load them on C-130 aircraft for transport to mortuary facilities. Not one of the wounded was brought in; MEDEVAC helicopters had taken them to various hospitals.

Late in the afternoon, the helicopter that had flown me to Tong Le Chon and had been shuttling supplies to the battle site landed, and the pilot told me that the battle was winding down and nearly over. He said that he was going to go up to the camp to get a cup of coffee and that then we would head back. A while later, he returned and suggested that I wait for one of the other helicopter crews to take me back; he was going back to the battlefield-landing zone to see if there was anything else he could do to help. After he and his crew left, I waited until about sunset for one of the other crews to finish their coffee and fly me back to Camp Widder. When we landed on a soccer field about a mile from camp, the pilot told me that he had not been able to make radio contact with anyone and that he had not been able to get me a ride. With that, he lifted off and left me to walk back to camp, walking in the dark in a heavy rain, carrying two large bags of supplies and my rifle.

By the time I got back to camp, I was half-mad that no one had come to get me and that everyone else was warm and dry in the mess hall but at least, I knew that I could get a good meal. Opening the door to my hooch, I nearly exploded. I was so mad; all of my belongings were piled up on the floor, and my bed had been stripped. I was furious and stomped over to the mess hall. As I walked in, a cheer went up. It turned out that the helicopter that I had originally been planning to fly back on had been shot down at the battlefield-landing zone. Everyone on board had been killed, and it was assumed that I was among them.

That was not all of the bad news that evening though. We got news that one of the Special Forces men from our camp had been killed that day. Once again, for reasons that escape me, God had allowed some of America's finest men to die that day, and yet He had again spared my life; I will always wonder why.

MY WAR, FIGHTING THE FRIENDLIES

As my year in Vietnam wound down, there were some very memorable events. One Saturday morning in July, I was sitting in the clubhouse located just outside of the camp compound, reading a book, when there was the sound of gunfire. Everyone ran to the camp, and, as soon as everyone was in, the gate was locked. I grabbed my flak jacket, helmet, and rifle and ran to my bunker. The firing picked up, and soon there was the sound of grenades exploding. From my bunker, there was nothing to see. After what seemed to be hours but was probably just about twenty minutes, we began to hear the command, "Cease fire! Cease fire!" A few minutes later, there was a request for a doctor to go to the airstrip. The American advisor for a Vietnamese-armored unit was calling for help; a number of his men had gotten in a firefight, and quite a few of them were wounded.

One of our men loaded up a jeep, and, as soon as someone could open the gate, we roared out and headed down to the airstrip. On the way, I noticed that a number of trees in the compound were down and that the front of the clubhouse had been knocked down. When we got to the airstrip and began dressing wounds and starting IV fluids, the

American advisor started calling for MEDEVAC helicopters. A few minutes later, the story became clear.

What had happened was that a Vietnamese-armored personnel carrier (APC) unit had camped the night before next to the airstrip. The unit commander had decided to go into town the next morning, and while he was there, he had gone to a bar. The commander of the Vietnamese LLDB unit located next to our camp was also in the bar. After a period of drinking, the two got into a fight, and the LLDB commander had reportedly knocked out the commander of the Vietnamese-armored personnel carrier unit. When the commander of that unit regained consciousness, he returned to the airstrip and ordered all of his men to move out with their APCs and set out to attack the LLDB camp. They mistakenly attacked our camp.

As the story was told, we realized that our people were responsible all for of those Vietnamese troops being shot. A few of our men had minor nicks from grenade fragments, but none had any significant wounds. Those with the small wounds were not eligible for the Purple Heart, since their wounds were not the result of enemy action but were from being attacked by the friendlies.

FORTY THOUSAND NVA!

Soon, I was to have a very unexpected experience. One of the SF sergeants was the advisor and leader of a small mercenary unit that was camped close to the town in a part of a rubber tree plantation. That unit was made up of Montagnard men, and it was a very special group of men. Each of these men was chosen because he had witnessed a family member being executed in a public display by the Viet Cong. Those men were said to be fierce fighters and were men who had a very personal hatred for the Viet Cong and the North Vietnamese. The SF sergeant came to me to tell me that I was invited to join them for a special occasion. The very primitive camp consisted of tarpaulins draped over parachute cord that had been stretched between trees. Under the very simple shelters were canvas cots, and that was the totality of their living quarters for the men and their families. In a central location was a campfire.

The sergeant explained that the men had invited me because I had taken care of their families at a time when most of them were quite sick. They had killed a water buffalo and would be having a big celebration. He also suggested that we eat and "enjoy" whatever they served and drink whatever they gave us. He told me that their rice wine tasted terrible, but I was to act as if it was great. The party went on for a couple of hours, and, yes, the rice wine was terrible. As the party seemed to be at its high point, the leader made a big show of bringing his daughter, who looked to be about thirteen years old, to give to me to be my wife. I asked the interpreter to tell him that I was very appreciative but that the US government would not allow me to take her as my wife and that I already had a wife back in the United States. I asked the interpreter to tell him that I thought she was very beautiful and would certainly make someone a wonderful wife. Whew! I got out of that, and everyone seemed to be happy.

About two weeks before I was to leave Vietnam, we were told that General Creighton Abrams would be visiting our camp. He arrived with several other high-ranking officers and spent the morning meeting with the camp's Special Forces officers. After lunch, they left. That evening, we were informed that an estimated forty thousand North Vietnamese soldiers surrounded our little camp of just over thirty men. The intelligence was that they were camped in the area around the town of Hon Quan and that they were planning a major offensive. General Abrams had promised to provide every possible resource if we were attacked. Major Menendez, our camp commander, told us that he wanted us to continue with our daily routines but that we were to sleep in our bunkers and suggested that we wear our flak jackets and helmets at night. Those next few days were quite tense.

Two weeks later, I boarded a single-engine de Havilland beaver and left for Ton Son Nhut and on for a trip back to the States. As the plane circled the town and gained altitude, I was glad to be heading home, but, at the same time, I felt guilty for leaving my friends behind. I knew that a big attack had to be coming, and, with regret, I knew that some of our hospital staff, many of the people from the town, and some of my friends would surely be killed. No one who has not had that experience can really know what I felt that day. During my year in Vietnam, everyone assumed that I was a good Christian, and, on Easter, Christmas, and for other special occasions, they always asked me to pray before the big meal. I assumed they were right. Whether they were right or not, as I looked down on Camp David Widder and the town of Hon Quan, I sure prayed for God to protect everyone.

A few months later, the country exploded with the big Tet offensive that spelled the beginning of the end for the US presence in South Vietnam.

STATESIDE AND ANGELS?

After arriving back in the US, my wife and I spent a few days with our families before heading for the next assignment, Charleston AFB, just outside of Charleston, South Carolina. One day before leaving, I developed bursitis in my right arm. The trip to Charleston involved driving through the Appalachian Mountains on very winding two-lane roads. The car was loaded down, and we were pulling a boat. Going up and down the mountains was pure misery. The car had a floor shift, and it seemed as if there must have been ten thousand times when I had to painfully shift and turn the steering wheel as we made it to more level land and straighter roads.

Within a few days after arriving in Charleston, we bought a house and settled in. The clinic at Charleston AFB was small but well-staffed, and the year there was enjoyable. In late March of 1968, we drove back to Louisville, Kentucky, to spend some time with family and friends. We called a friend who had been stationed with me at MacDill AFB, in Tampa, Florida, and made plans to spend a night with him and his wife in Atlanta, Georgia, on our way back to Charleston. On April 4, 1968, Martin Luther King, Jr. was killed. A couple of days later, we drove to Atlanta for a reunion with Dr. Joel Smith and his wife, Carolyn. That evening, we were to go out to eat, and Joel decided to drive us by Ebenezer Baptist Church, where Dr. King's body would be brought the next day. To this day, I still remember that building.

After eating, Joel suggested that we go to a nightclub for an after dinner drink. We parked on the street about fifty yards from the nightclub, and as soon as we got out of the car, a man came walking down the sidewalk toward us. He was dressed in a Pinkerton's uniform and was twirling a wooden baton. When he got close, he asked what we were doing, and we told him that we were going to the nightclub. He said, "You must want a drink awfully bad." At that point, he told us, "Look up and down the street, and you will see that you have the only car on the street that still has a windshield." Then he asked if we knew what was going on and told us that the whole city of Atlanta was caught up in a race riot brought on by the murder of Martin Luther King. He had us look around and pointed out the flames from buildings burning all around the city—flames that literally lighted up the sky. He told us that the governor had called out the National Guard, and he suggested that we go home as quickly as possible. We thanked him, got in the car, and Joel headed home.

After driving only a short distance, we passed a motel and, a couple of blocks later, made a left turn. We had gone less than a block when the rotor in his car's distributor broke and the engine stopped. To say the least, we were horrified. Joel and I got out. We could see flames rising up into the sky all around us. There were sirens everywhere, and National Guard trucks were roaring past us. We came up with a plan. That part of Atlanta was hilly, and two streets we had been driving on had required us to go uphill. It seemed that we could let the car roll backward to the intersection, turn and roll downhill and into the parking lot of the motel that we had passed. Then we could check into the motel and could safely spend the night there.

Joel began backing down to the intersection, and, as he turned, he turned too soon. The back tire jumped the curb, and we were stuck with the front tire on one side of the corner and the back tire on the other side. As Joel and I got out, all I could think of was that here we were in the middle of a riot with both of our wives and that Carolyn was pregnant. Suddenly, a car screeched to a halt, and five big black men got out and came running toward us. I know that they were not ten feet tall, but in my mind they looked that big. As the first one got near, he yelled out, "You are in big trouble. We have got to help you!" With that, two of them grabbed the front bumper and lifted the car up and over the curb. They then told us to let the car roll back to the motel parking lot. When we made it to the parking lot, one of them told Joel to go call his brother to come get us, and then they stood guard until Joel's brother arrived to take us to the safety of Joel's home. As we got in the car, the men left.

Those men had a profound effect on my life. I knew that they had risked their lives to save us and knew that I had no right to ever again harbor prejudice toward anyone. I owed those men a huge debt of gratitude. In fact, that was the reason I volunteered to run a cancer and cervical dysplasia clinic for indigent patients, most of whom were black. I did that for thirty-two years, and it was the most rewarding part of my medical practice. Forty-seven years later, I related the story to Phoebe Dawson, the former director of New Beginnings Adoption Agency and the person who had arranged for the adoption of two of our daughters. She looked at me and asked me why it had taken so long for me to realize that those men were very possibly angels. I'll never know, but the debt I owe them can never be repaid.

RESIDENCY

I remember my excitement when I learned that I had been accepted for a residency in obstetrics and gynecology at the Medical College of South Carolina in Charleston, South Carolina. I had already been accepted at several other university programs, but none appealed to me as much as the program in Charleston. The residency in Charleston had the advantage of having faculty members who were well-known for their work in each of the subspecialties. The Charleston area had a large indigent population, and while rampant poverty would not seem to be a plus, it meant that there would be no shortage of patients in need of the services offered by the county hospital and the university hospital. The interns, residents, and the specialists who made up the faculty would treat all those patients. The Obstetrics and Gynecology had a great academic reputation, and a part of that was the result of Dr. Hester, the chairman of the department, requiring that every one of the interns and residents attend the department's lectures four days each week. I loved Charleston, a beautiful and very historic place. All in all, there just couldn't have been a better place to spend four years of residency training.

The other two first year residents were William McLean and Charles Stamey. Both of them had also served in the armed forces, and the three of us soon became close friends. During the first year, residents stayed busy delivering babies, assisting in the operating room, and managing patients on the postpartum and gynecology floors in both the Medical College Hospital and the Charleston County Hospital. For four mornings each week, we saw patients in the clinics. With each successive year, the residents were given more responsibility and were tasked with performing more difficult surgical cases. By the fourth year, the residents officially became teaching fellows. At that point, most of our time in the operating room was spent teaching and assisting second and third year residents as they performed surgery. Fourth year residents had the option of being the primary surgeon on many of the more difficult cases. Two of our faculty members, Dr. Paul Underwood and Dr. E. J. (Billy) Dennis, were most often the lead surgeons on radical cancer operations.

By the second year, we were allowed to moonlight (work in other hospital emergency rooms) when we were off of duty. From the second year on, the extra money earned by moonlighting was spent learning to fly. During residency, the time that was not spent at the hospital moonlighting and learning to fly was spent reading. I read and reread every textbook I could find and nearly every article in several professional journals. During the third year, my second son was born. I don't remember spending any of my spare time with my wife and almost never made an effort to do anything with her. Fourth year residents were allowed to take call from home, but, instead of going to bed, I would often drive back in to check in at the emergency room and make late-night rounds. I did that so often that someone put a sign on my locker that said, "Night Stalker." I did make it a point to go to church Sunday, and even took over the youth program, but, in retrospect, I almost never tried to do anything with my wife.

God has often acted to give me a special blessing, even when I didn't really know him and didn't realize the blessing until years later. One of our clinical rotations was on the endocrinology service headed by Dr. Oliver Williamson. While I was on that rotation, Dr. Williamson was gone for a period of time, and the service was rather slow during his absence. Dr. Hester, the chairman of the Obstetrics and Gynecology Department, called me into his office. He explained that two doctors, Catherine and Reginald Hamblin, were planning to spend a few days in Charleston, South Carolina. The Hamblins were from Australia and New Zealand, and while they were serving as medical missionaries in Ethiopia, they had met and married. There they saw a great many women who had experienced excessively long labors and could not deliver their baby. The pressure of the baby's head while in the birth canal would eventually cut off the blood supply to areas of the vagina and bladder and, on some occasions, cut off the blood supply to areas of the vagina and rectum. Eventually, those women were carried on makeshift stretchers until they eventually reached a hospital where a cesarean section delivery was done. Usually, the baby was born dead. A result of the prolonged labor and pressure from the baby's head was that the tissues lost blood supply and died. That tissue necrosis would leave large fistulas (openings that connected the bladder or rectum with the vagina). Those women were unable to keep themselves clean, no one could stand to be with them, and they usually ended up living on the street. Recognizing that surgical repair of the fistulas would lead to a failure to heal, unless a tissue flap could be used to bring in a new blood supply, the Hamblin's developed surgical techniques that resulted in a 95 percent cure rate. They developed a fistula hospital in Addis Ababa, Ethiopia, that has provided corrective surgery to more than 32,000 women.

Dr. Hester asked me to not only spend a few days showing them the city of Charleston but also asked me to get together with other residents to find some patients with fistulas. We did find two patients, and I was given the opportunity to assist in surgery and learn the techniques developed by the Hamblins. I had no idea that those days spent with Reginald and Catherine Hamblin would eventually result in some truly miserable patients being helped as I used the knowledge passed on to me by two of the world's greatest humanitarians.

During my residency, the state of South Carolina did what many other states did. The legislature passed a law that made it legal for a woman to get an abortion for the health of the mother. After that, women would come to the clinic wanting an abortion. The receptionist would send them to the psychiatry office, where someone would give them a note saying, "This patient needs an abortion for reasons of their mental health." As far as we knew, none of the women were ever seen by a psychiatrist or clinical psychologist; that was just a way of getting around the law and making it possible for any woman to conveniently get an abortion. Even though I had originally thought abortion was wrong, I didn't have any absolute standard of right and wrong, I began to help with the work load by doing abortions. By the end of my fourth year, I even gave a talk in which I made the argument that as many abortions as possible should be done on poorer women so that there would not be so many children added to the welfare rolls. I even made the argument that fewer schools would be necessary and spoke of how the taxpayers would benefit from increasing the abortion rate.

All of my hours of study began to pay off. We had to take an in-training exam: I was really proud to find out that I had gotten the top score in the country. After completing residency, we took the American Board of Obstetrics and Gynecology written exam. Again, I was told that I had done very well and that the rumor was that I had gotten the top score in the country. I was ready for private practice and was filled with pride.

A BOX OF KLEENEX

As the four years of residency drew to an end, I began to look at opportunities. I remembered how much fun it had been living in Tampa, Florida, while I was stationed at MacDill Air Force Base. Throughout my residency, the plan was to return to Florida to practice. I flew down to visit several places to select the best opportunity and discovered something about myself: I had changed, and Florida no longer held any appeal for me.

Next, I made a trip to visit with a friend in Bowling Green, Kentucky, and spent a few hours with an obstetrician/gynecologist there. When I returned home, Kentucky seemed to be calling me. A few days later, I went outside to wash my car. Before turning on the hose, the process of cleaning the inside began. The car had bucket seats, and there was a space between the seats. A box of Kleenex occupied that space. As I picked up the box to vacuum under it, I suddenly realized that the box in my hand had been there since the day I finished my internship and left Ohio six years earlier. That was when I remembered that I had needed to take allergy shots twice a week since age six during the time I was living in Kentucky, Indiana, and Ohio. I remembered that every day I would wake up with my eyes swollen shut and my nose running and that I sneezed incessantly.

When I left for school or for work, I would need to take two of the small packets of tissues and always kept a box of Kleenex in the car. That box would only last me about six to seven days. While vacuuming the car, I suddenly realized that the box in my hand had lasted six years and was still full, allergy shots had not been needed since leaving Kentucky and Ohio, and I only had problems with allergies when I went back to Kentucky to visit. At that moment, it became clear that going back to Kentucky was out of the question. A couple of days later, I asked my fellow resident, Chuck Stamey, what he thought about me going with him to Columbus, Georgia, and going into practice together. Looking back, many people asked me what had caused me to move to Georgia; it was always fun to look them in the eye and tell them that I had made that decision because of a box of Kleenex.

THANK GOD I FAILED

A few weeks before finishing my residency, it was time to sell the house and look at buying a house in Columbus. Before heading in to the hospital one morning, I picked up a piece of cardboard and wrote "FOR SALE" on it and stapled it to a tree in front of the house. About two hours later, someone called, and, in five minutes, he had bought the house. Within weeks, we had a house in Columbus, and my family had moved in. The next few weeks, I lived with a fellow resident in downtown Charleston as I waited to finish my residency.

My first day in Columbus was a Saturday. I had offered to be the on call attending physician that day. I was broken in fast. By suppertime, I had already done five cesarean section deliveries in addition to scrubbing in with the family practice residents on several other deliveries. Dr. Souma, the chief of the Obstetrics and Gynecology Department, knew of my interest in gynecologic cancer and had already scheduled a radical hysterectomy for cervical cancer. Again, that was a busy day in the operating room. I was excited to be in Columbus.

Before moving to Columbus, Georgia, Dr. Stamey and I had arranged to have an office built, and, for us, it was perfect. As a student at the University of Louisville, I had come to love the school colors—red and black—so my own private office was decorated with red walls, and I had three black chairs to finish out my consulting office. On the first Thursday, a patient sat down in my office and told me, "I love your office, I'm a professional prostitute." I really didn't quite know how to take that statement; nevertheless, I still liked my choice of colors.

I found that the Columbus area was just what I wanted. I had a busy practice, everyone at the hospital treated me like a king, and there was great hunting close to where I lived. In fact, there was just too much to do to find time to spend with my wife and two sons. Then, about the time that we found out that my wife was pregnant with our third child, I became involved in an affair. For a period of time, it was possible to keep the affair secret, but eventually the secret was out.

He never told me the reason, but I think that Chuck (Dr. Stamey) had just put up with me as long as he could and decided to pull out and join another group of doctors. Chuck was one of the best physicians I have ever known, and, even to this day, the dissolution of our practice has bothered me. That began the series of events that forever changed my life.

About the time Chuck moved his practice, I was preparing to take my oral Obstetrics and Gynecology board exam. There was no question that I would ace that exam; hadn't I scored really high on my written exams? While this was going on, my marriage had gotten really rocky. I will never forget my oral board exam. The exam was in Chicago. I sat down in a large room with about fifty other nervous candidates. When my name was called, I looked up and saw that my examiner was Dr. Richard Mattingly. Dr. Mattingly was well-known by the residents and faculty at The Medical University of South Carolina Obstetrics and

Gynecology Department. Dr. Hester, the chairman of the department, had never had one of his residents fail the oral exam, unless the examiner was Dr. Mattingly. Even worse, the scuttlebutt was that Dr. Mattingly had never passed any of Dr. Hester's residents. I became one more of those causalities. Dr. Mattingly started out by asking me about the Stein-Leventhal syndrome. Then he asked me where the name for the syndrome originated. Next, he asked whether the syndrome was named for one man or two. The next question was where those two men did their practice, what the street address of their offices or office was, and whether or not they were in practice together. By then, I was angry; I knew he was determined that another of Dr. Hester's residents would not get by him. Weeks passed, and eventually the letter from the American Board of Obstetrics and Gynecology arrived with the news that I failed the oral section of my board exams. I was devastated.

Later, I sold my pickup truck and was cleaning out all my collected junk. One of the items that I threw out onto the ground was a rope. My son, Matt, was just old enough to be speaking short sentences, and, when he saw the rope, he said, "Dat a rope, dat da rope hospital man use to tie my daddy up." That statement hurt. The truth was that most of the times when I had called my wife to tell her that I was tied up at the hospital, I was with the other woman.

Soon afterward, my wife had me served with separation papers and filed for divorce, and the other woman involved in my affair began to date someone else. The practice partnership with Dr. Stamey dissolving, failing my oral board exam, the impending divorce, being rejected, and the possibility of loosing my sons through divorce all caused me to become very depressed. I became suicidal. I even picked out a large boulder overlooking a creek, went there several times to rehearse my suicide, and had decided that I would sit on that rock and commit suicide by shooting myself just above my right ear.

Somehow, I knew that I should make, at least, one attempt to seek help. I couldn't bring myself to make an appointment with a psychiatrist; I couldn't let anyone in the medical community know that I had a problem. I did know that David Howle, the pastor at Edgewood Baptist Church in Columbus, did some counseling. Since he didn't know me, it seemed safe enough to go see him. I still joke with him about the fact that he was the worse counselor I have ever met. He wasn't interested in my problems; he was only interested in my problem, my sin problem. He told me that the Bible says that all have sinned and come short of the glory of God and that Jesus had suffered and was crucified for my sins. He explained that if I would repent, turn from my sins, and ask Jesus to be my Lord and Savior, then my sins would be forgiven, and I would be saved from eternal damnation. Something happened—David Roberts, who had never cried, even when injured or hurt, began to confess and weep. I prayed to receive Jesus as my Lord and Savior. I had heard the Gospel many times and had thought that I was a Christian, but, on my knees in David Howle's office, I was forever changed. In fact, now I cry at everything—I am even crying as I write this.

When I left the church, I really didn't know what had happened, but there was an overwhelming feeling of peace. An all-encompassing desire to read the Bible took over, and I looked forward to having patients in labor; then the many hours spent in the hospital would be my time to read the Gideon bibles that had been placed in each of the physician call rooms.

After praying to receive Christ and becoming a member of Edgewood Baptist Church, I was baptized. God began to convict me of many things; one of the issues was that I needed to go apologize to my wife, ask her to allow me to begin dating her, and tell her that I wanted our marriage put back together. I went to her and told her that if we would allow God to be in charge, it would work. She had no reason to trust me—her trust had been broken so many times—and she turned me down. Soon after that, the divorce became final, and she remarried.

ABORTIONS AND ME

I had continued doing abortions and thought that I was helping women. In January, just a few months after becoming a Christian, our associate pastor, Andy Merritt, gave a sermon on the subject of abortion. I listened intently and took notes. As he went through his sermon, he spoke about the many verses that told of the value God puts on human life. He began with the story of how God created man and woman. He referenced Psalm 139:13–16, where the psalmist speaks of how God formed him in his mother's womb and knew every detail of his body. Pastor Merritt cited Genesis 4:8–11, where Cain killed his brother Abel, and God told Cain that the voice of his brother's blood cried out to God from the ground. Then the question was asked: How much more does the blood of millions of babies cry out to God today? And if Cain was cursed because of the murder of his brother, how can God ignore the fact that we in the United States have killed millions of babies by abortion?

I thought that Andy was out of his mind and believed that when I was aborting pregnant women, I was doing a good thing and helping them. I went home after that service and began studying the Bible to prepare my argument. I would go back and show that young pastor that he was wrong. About an hour into my study session, I realized that

I was wrong; God had not given me the right to kill babies. I knew immediately that I had to stop doing abortions.

That night, sleep came very late; one reason after another came to mind as to why I could not quit doing abortions. The first reason was my friends would think I was crazy. Another was the question; how could I tell my office staff and my patients about the reason for my decision? Finally, I couldn't put out of my mind the fact that the divorce had left me with a lot of expenses and that the money from doing abortions was all that was keeping me afloat. The more I came up with reasons to continue doing abortions, the more I knew I had to quit. Sometime in the early morning hours, I kneeled by my bed, prayed, and told God that if I quit doing abortions and it caused me to go bankrupt, then I would just go bankrupt, but I would do what I had to do.

The next morning after going to my office, I told my receptionist that if I had anyone scheduled for an abortion, she was to call them and tell them that they would have to see someone else, that Dr. Roberts had quit doing abortions. I also told her that if there were any appointments scheduled with patients wanting abortions, those patients would have to see someone else. Finally, if any calls came in asking about abortions, the callers were to be told that Dr. Roberts didn't do abortions. She looked at me in shock, stood up, hugged me, and said, "You don't know how long I have been praying for this moment."

To my surprise, that month was the busiest month I had experienced since starting my practice and brought in more money than any month before then. It was obvious that God was blessing the decision that followed Andy Merritt's sermon. Even more surprising was that it really wasn't hard to tell others about that.

One year after I had failed my oral board exam, I took the exam for a second time. It was a pleasant experience that time, and I passed. Today, I am so thankful that Dr. Mattingly had been one of my examiners the first time I took the exam and that I had failed it. That, along with some other things, finally broke me; the resultant depression was what God used to bring me to my knees and to introduce me to Jesus Christ, my Lord and Savior.

About a year later, I discovered that the city of Columbus, Georgia, was funding an abortion clinic run by The Medical Center Hospital. As a municipal hospital, city tax money was also being used to support a section of the hospital that was set aside for the care of those patients having second and early third trimester abortions. That fact was shared with a couple of other pro-life physicians and with one of the city councilmen who was a pro-life Christian. We met several times, and the councilman, John Wells, drew up a referendum that would stop the city from using tax revenue to fund abortions.

The day that the referendum was to be presented, the council chamber was packed with people who were there to show their support for the measure. After Mr. Wells read his referendum, a good many of us were allowed to speak. The council then voted with eleven to one against the measure, with only Mr. Wells voting for it. We were all devastated. There was some talk in the weeks and months that followed that a number of women's prayer groups had been formed and were praying that God would stop what was happening in Columbus with regard to the city funding abortions. I kept praying that God would show me what I should do, but nothing ever came to mind.

When a physician is granted hospital privileges, he or she is automatically a member of a department staff, depending on their specialty. The Obstetrics and Gynecology department at the Medical Center hospital elected new officers every two years. While it sounds like an honor to be elected chairman of a hospital department, in actuality, the position requires attendance at a great many meetings and requires spending a great many hours dealing with administrative duties. No one wants to be elected chairman of a hospital department. All of us always made it a point to try to be present at the meeting when officers were to be elected so that one of us could nominate an absent department member, who was not there to defend themselves. Of course, that absent person would be elected and saddled with the job. One evening, while I was delivering a baby, my name was placed in nomination, and I got stuck with the job.

About one week after being elected as the chairman, the assistant hospital administrator called. He began by saying that he needed me to do him a favor. I agreed to try to help. Then he said, "Nobody is coming to the abortion clinic any longer, and no second trimester abortions are being done in the hospital. It is costing us a fortune to staff the clinic, and that hospital abortion unit has to be staffed around the clock. We just can't afford to keep those units open. Since you are the chairman of the Obstetrics and Gynecology Department, I have to have your permission to close those units." I laughed and asked him if he knew my stand on abortion. He said that he did but that he still had to have my permission. I again laughed and gave him my permission. At that moment, I knew why God had not shown me anything that I was to do; he had done it.

As time passed, there were patients who came in seeking help for depression. Many of those were women who told of bouts of depression that happened two times each year. On careful questioning, they related the fact that they had previously undergone an abortion. Then they talked about experiencing depression each year as the anniversary of their abortion neared. They also realized that they also became very depressed each year at what would have been that aborted baby's birthday. The knowledge of what was happening to them was helpful. Most of the time, I suggested to them that they accept the fact that their suffering was God's way to get their attention. I would often find that women were open to a further spiritual discussion. We would talk about the fact that I had done abortions but that God had forgiven me and He was waiting with open arms to accept them and forgive them. My recommendation would then be for them to pray and confess that what they had done was sin and turn to the Lord Jesus to ask Him to forgive them. If they would do that, they could know for certain that Christ had forgiven them and that they could forgive themselves. We would then discuss the need for them to talk with their pastor—perhaps, name the aborted baby and have a private memorial service. One patient would just not leave until I had prayed with her; she prayed the Sinner's Prayer, and, as one experiencing salvation, she left with a new peace and with the knowledge that she was one of God's saved children.

In years to come, that message was one that I was able to give in many churches, and, to my surprise, I was often invited to speak in churches belonging to denominations different from the one that of my affiliation. Any time I have that opportunity, I always make it a point to remind people that with the millions of babies that have been aborted in the United States since the Roe v. Wade decision, there are millions of men and women who have been involved in abortion. Then the next point is always that, "If you are one of those who are suffering guilt and depression resulting from your involvement in an abortion, please realize that God has forgiven me and He is waiting to forgive you."

LIFE GOES ON

One Sunday evening, just before the church service was to begin, Mike Sims, one of the unmarried family practice residents, came in with a very pretty lady named Cindy, and the two of them sat down by me. My thought was that he had finally found the right woman. Just then, he got up, walked to the back of the church, and returned with another young lady. The one he had brought in first was to eventually become my wife. When people ask me where I met my wife, the thought that comes to me is that just as God brought Eve to Adam, He brought her to me and sat her down in a pew beside me.

The most interesting part of the story is that she had been married to one of the family practice residents in Columbus, and the marriage had ended in divorce as a result of his involvement with another woman. While the affair was ongoing, Cindy became pregnant. During the pregnancy, she heard about all of the terrible things that the awful Dr. David Roberts had done. As the time for her to deliver approached, she found out that her doctor was going out of town and that Dr. Roberts would be covering his practice. She asked to have her labor induced in order to keep from being delivered by that terrible Dr. Roberts. Later, she learned that I had become a Christian while my divorce was proceeding and that I had even asked my ex-wife to date me and put our marriage back together. She had also learned that my ex-wife, Jackie, remarried very quickly after the divorce. It is even more amazing that the woman, who had asked to have her labor induced to avoid having to deal with that awful Dr. Roberts, is now my wife.

Kelly, the daughter who was born as a result of the induced labor, later asked if she could become a Roberts and become my second of my four adopted children. A few years later, we adopted Katie, and, two and a half years later, a full sister, Kiersten, was born and placed with us, making a total of six children.

One night, I finished speaking at a prenatal class, and, while driving home, there was a loud bang. Someone had fired a shotgun loaded with buckshot, and the buckshot had not only made several holes in the passenger side door but also two windows on the passenger side were blown out. As soon as I got home, I called the police and was asked, "Did you stop?" My reply was, "Not me, I learned in Vietnam to keep going." Again, I was not even hurt.

During our time in Columbus, Georgia, we were able to make two short-term mission trips to work in Tenwek Hospital in Kenya and Sanyati Baptist Hospital in Zimbabwe. During the time at Sanyati Baptist Hospital, every day, I saw patients who had various forms of vesicovaginal and rectovaginal fistulas. Back during my residency, no one would have ever thought that I would someday be at a Christian mission hospital in Africa using the skills taught to me by the two Dr. Hamblins.

When Katie was ten and a half years old, a nurse asked me if we had any plans for the springtime school break. As the discussion progressed, she suggested that we try skiing at Red Lodge, Montana, and said that Red Lodge was her favorite town in the whole world. I had never heard of the place, but, when I checked, there really was a Red Lodge and there really was a ski area there. We made it to Red Lodge, but, after two days, Katie's ski boots were hurting her, and she didn't want to ski anymore. The next day, Katie and I took Cindy and Kiersten up to the ski area and returned to Red Lodge to do the town. It didn't take long to see a town of 2,300 people.

We stopped to get hot chocolate and coffee and walked out to enjoy a beautiful spring day. Next to the coffee shop was a real estate office. We were looking at some pictures of property when Lorie Davis, one of the real estate agents, introduced herself, and, after a short conversation, she offered to show us the area. After looking at several places, she showed us one piece of undeveloped land that had a creek and a view of the mountains. Katie began to run around and kept saying, "Dad, look at this." Sensing her excitement, I asked her if she wanted me to buy the place and build a house there. When she said yes, I made an offer. Then we had to drive up to the ski lodge and tell Cindy what we had just done. Cindy's brother is an architect in Bozeman, Montana, and Cindy had always wanted him to build us a house. So, when she thought about being close to her brother and having him build her a house, she liked the idea, and I got away with buying property without even talking with her.

After building a house outside of Red Lodge, we used it for two years as a vacation home. During those two years, I met Dr. William Philips, the president of Yellowstone Baptist College in Billings, Montana. He asked me to be the first speaker in their new chapel, and, not long after that, we agreed that I would become the vice president of Institutional Development at the college. Prior to finalizing that agreement, I really was not sure whether it would be feasible, since the position paid so much less than I earned practicing medicine. While I was sleeping, these words, "But my God shall supply all your needs…" (Philippians 4:19), came to mind. I woke up knowing that I should accept Dr. Philips's offer. A few months later, I closed my medical practice, and we moved to Red Lodge, where for the next five years I made the commute of fifty-five miles each way to work at the college and to teach biology. I left after five years to what I thought would be retirement.

LaVie is an organization that consists of two crisis pregnancy centers in Billings, Montana. For six years, it was a privilege to serve on the board of directors for that organization. Early one morning on the way to a board meeting, I was driving in on a highway covered with about two inches of fresh powdery snow. Each time a truck would approach from the opposite direction, the snow would swirl and produce what is known as a *whiteout*. I was following a truck that was throwing up a cloud of snow, and, coming from the opposite direction, there was another large truck followed by a pickup truck. As we passed on the highway, the other pickup truck and my vehicle were caught in total whiteout conditions with zero visibility. When I could finally see something, there were two headlights that were headed straight toward the headlights of my vehicle. Somehow, the other driver and I each swerved to the right and managed to avoid a head-on collision. Once again, God had saved my life and had saved the driver of the oncoming pickup truck.

After retiring for the second time, I went back to work as an adjunct instructor at the Rocky Mountain College Physician Assistant Program in Billings, Montana. At that time, the program was short-staffed, and when the program was fully staffed, my time at Rocky ended. Then in 2013 when my time on the board of directors of the LaVie crisis pregnancy centers in Billings, Montana, was over, I took a part-time position there—an opportunity to be an active part of an amazing ministry where unborn babies' lives are saved and men and women hear the Gospel of Jesus.

As of this time, I have made three mission trips to Peru. In January of 2014, and at the invitation of the OB/GYN faculty of Trujillo Regional Hospital in Trujillo, Peru, I had the opportunity to present lectures about the repair of vesicovaginal and rectovaginal fistulas and lectures on the subject of necrotizing fasciitis. At the beginning of the lectures, I was able to give my testimony and present the Gospel. After three mission trips to Peru, that place and the people have a part of my heart. What's next: more trips to Peru, where I will be doing some teaching, sharing of the Gospel, and speaking in other places and sharing the story of my conversion from performing abortions. That will be an opportunity to speak about God's love for every one of his children and His love for those whose lives have been damaged by their involvement in an abortion.

I have often been involved in situations where I could have been killed and have wondered why God allowed me to live. Will there be more of those life or death events? Will one of those events get me? Maybe, but it will be okay.

What will the future hold? I still wonder, but I keep telling Him, "Lord, if there is something you want me to do, let me know. With your strength and your provision, I'll do it. I'm old and ugly, but I'm not dead yet."

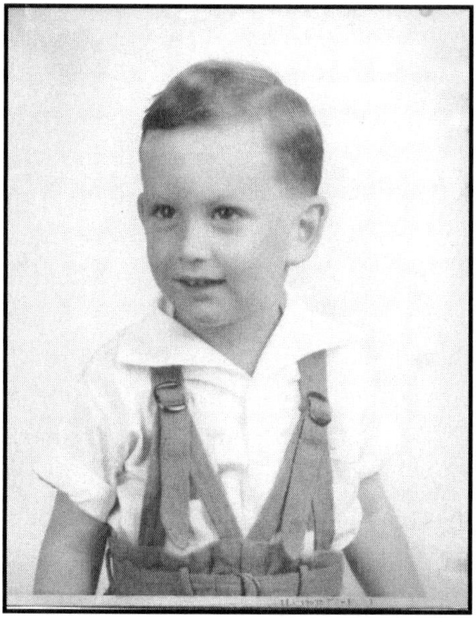

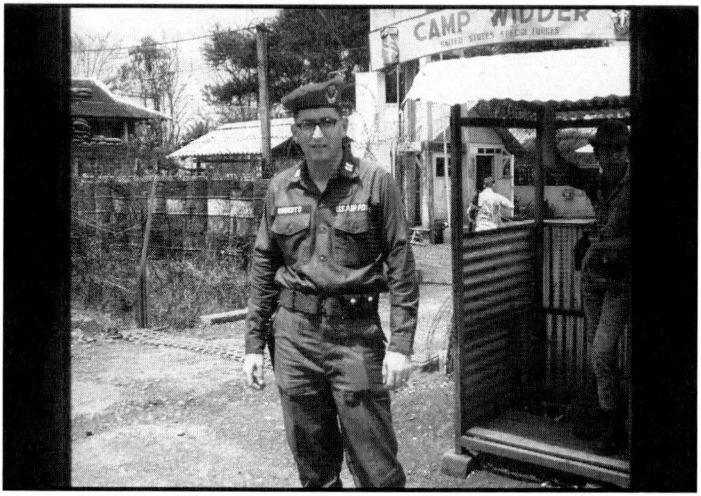
CAMP
UNITED STATES SPECIAL FORCES

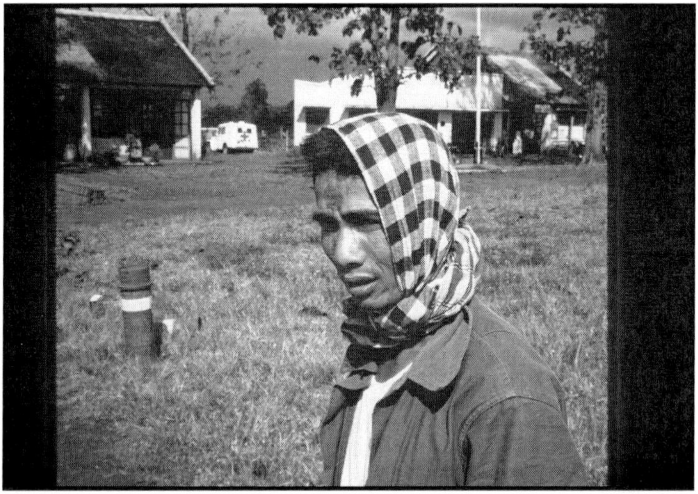

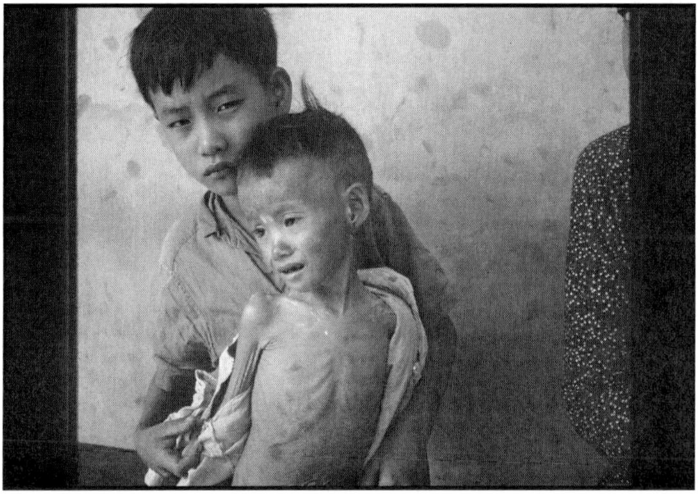

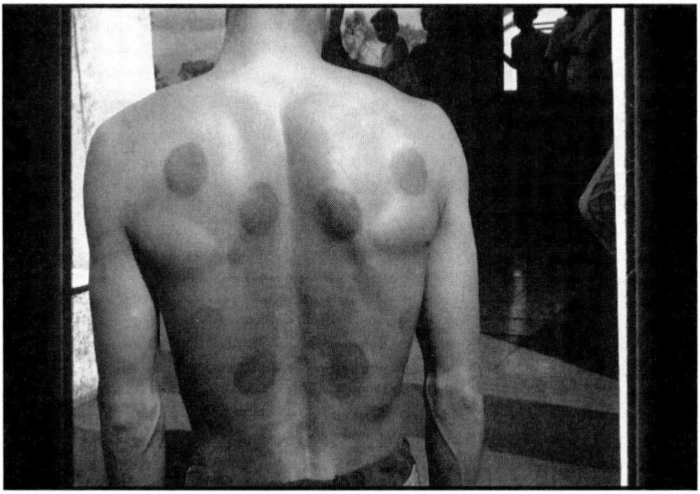

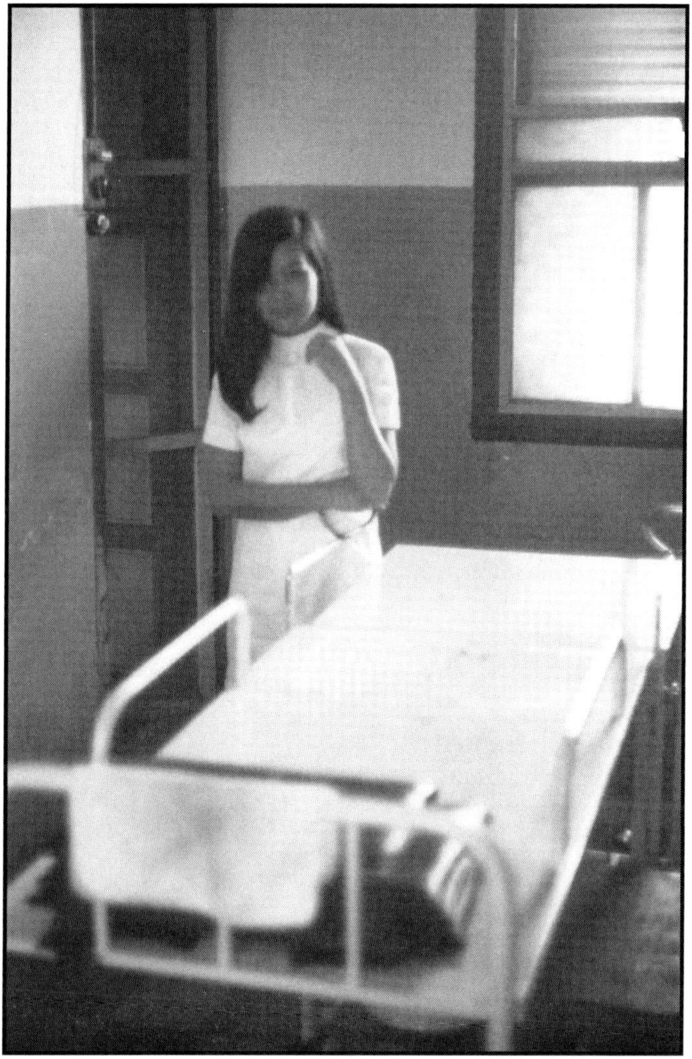

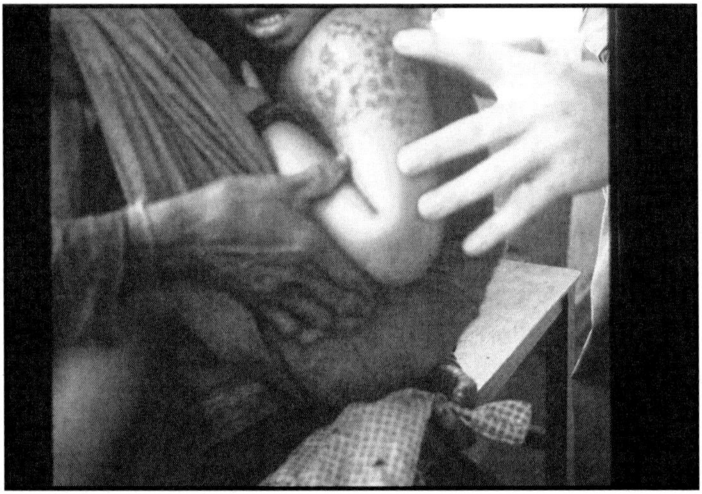

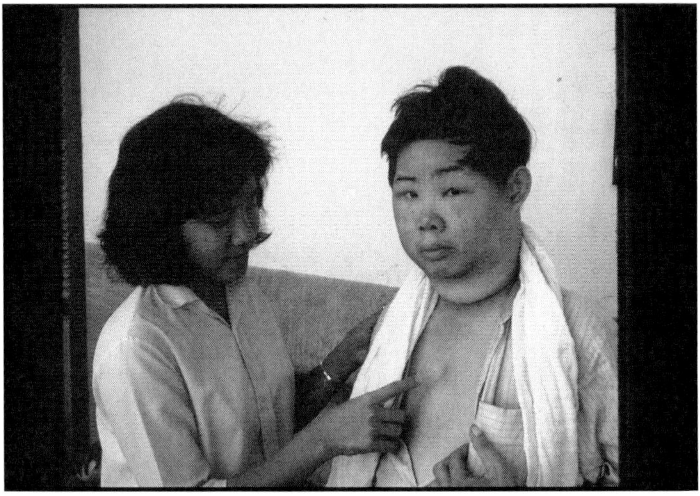

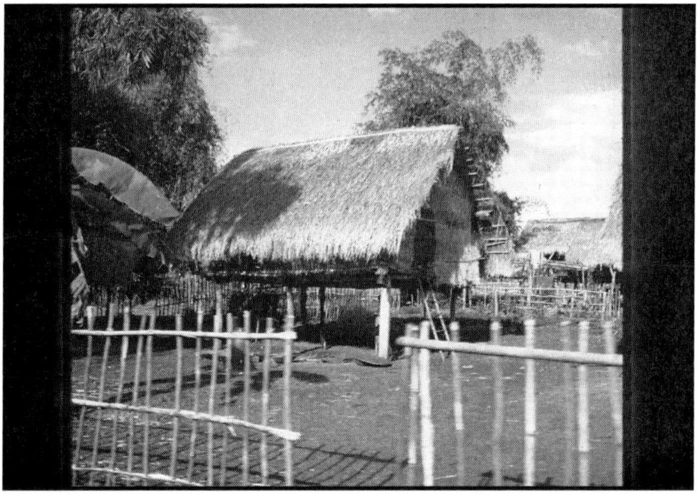

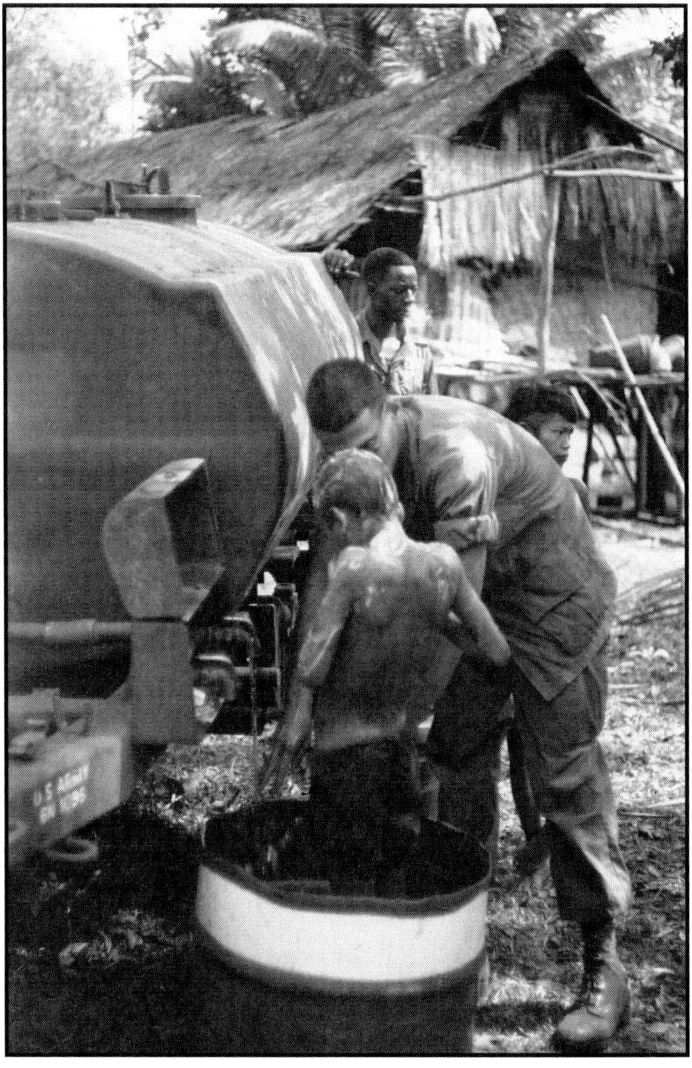
U.S. ARMY

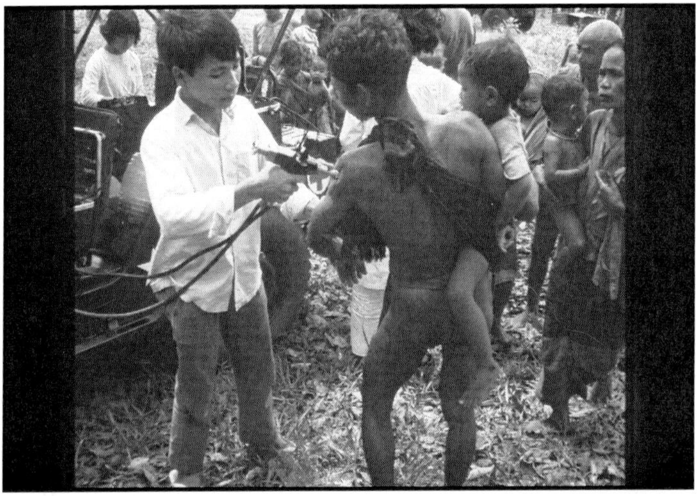

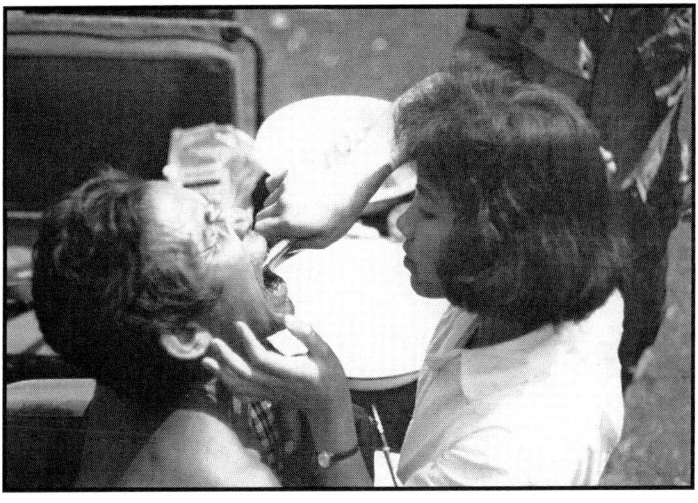

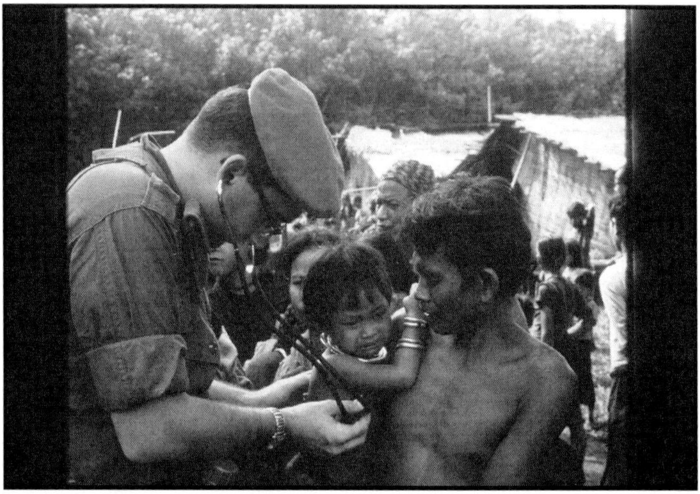

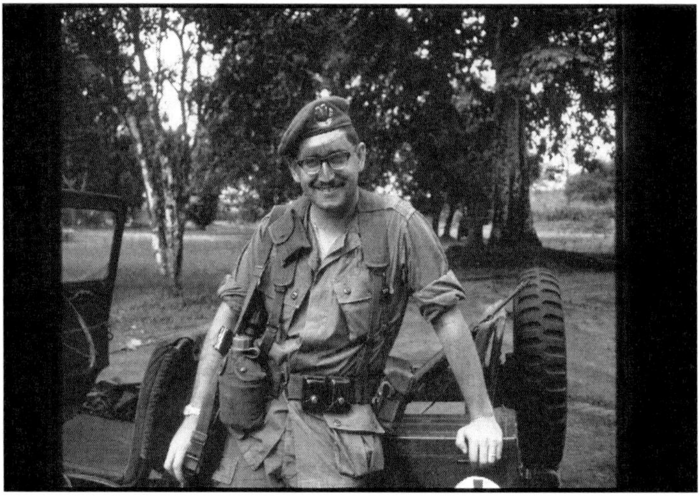

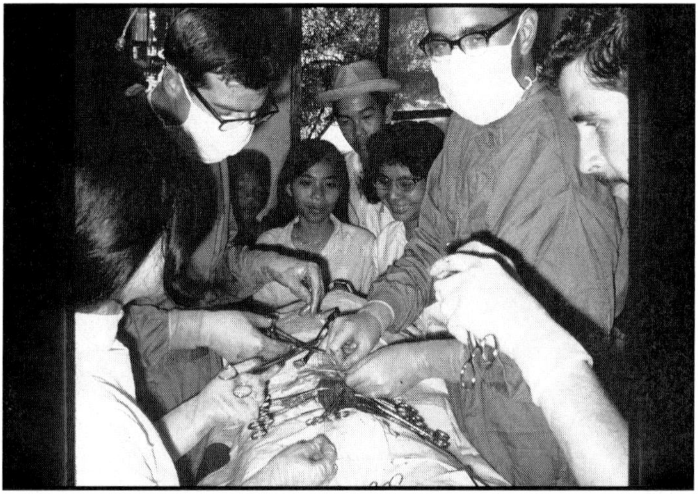

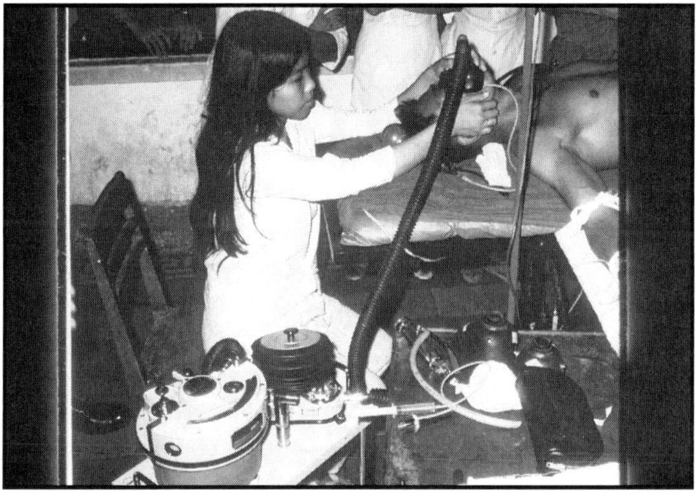

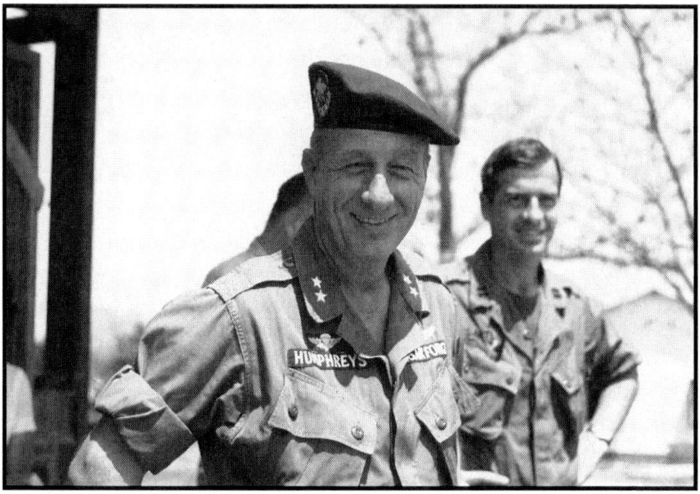
HUMPHREYS

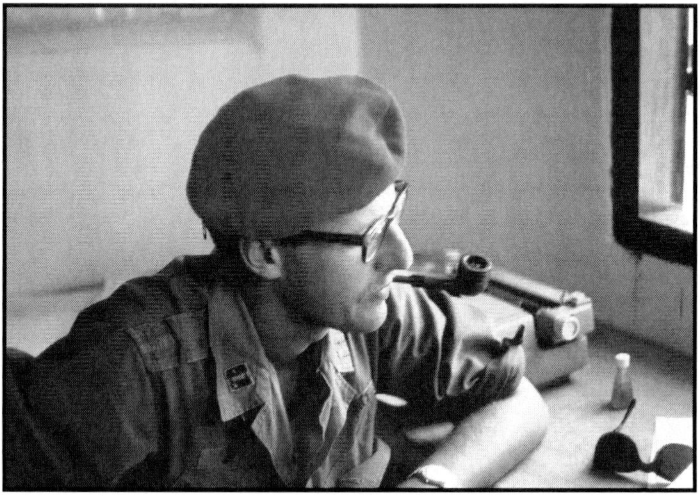

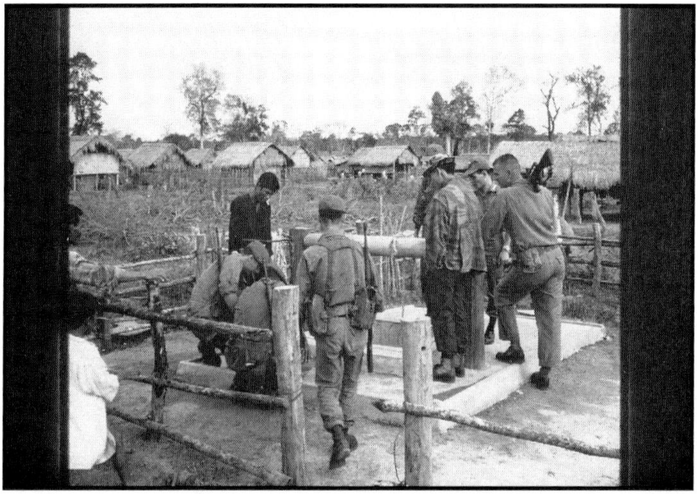

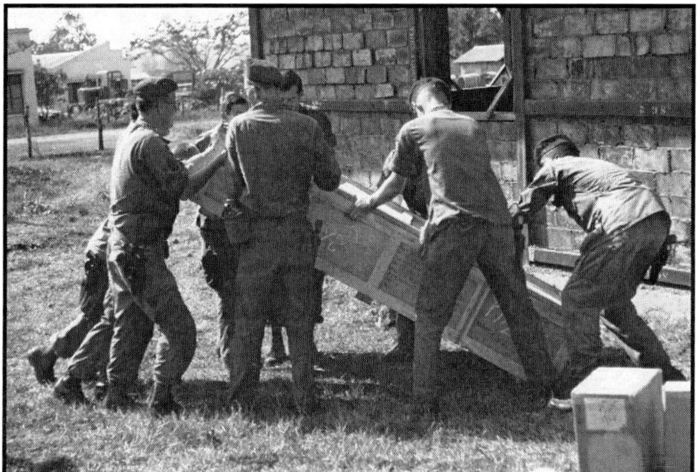

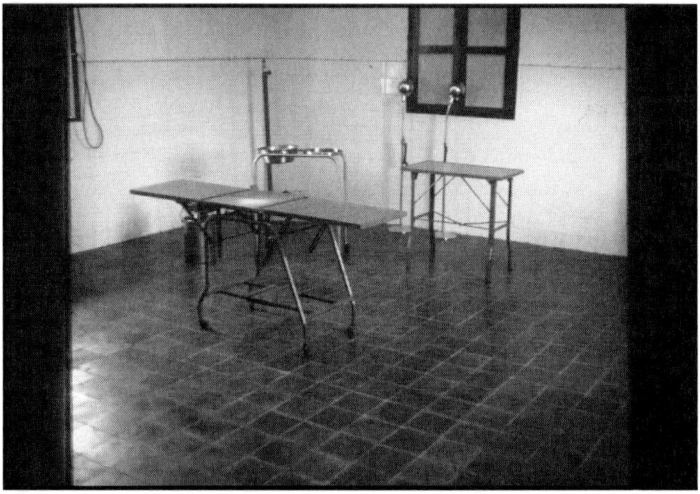

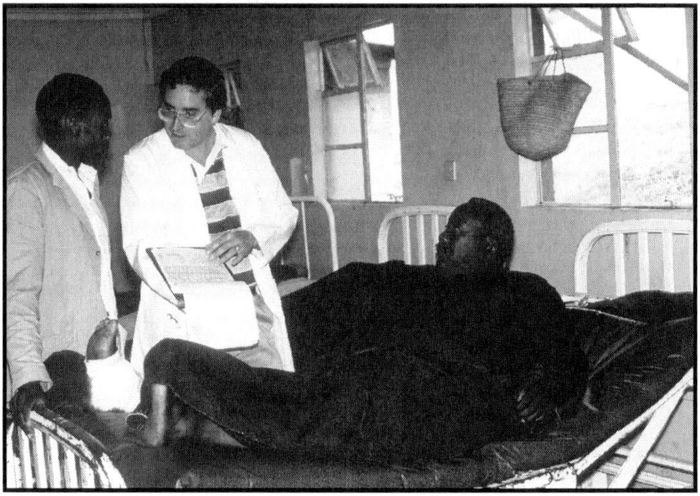

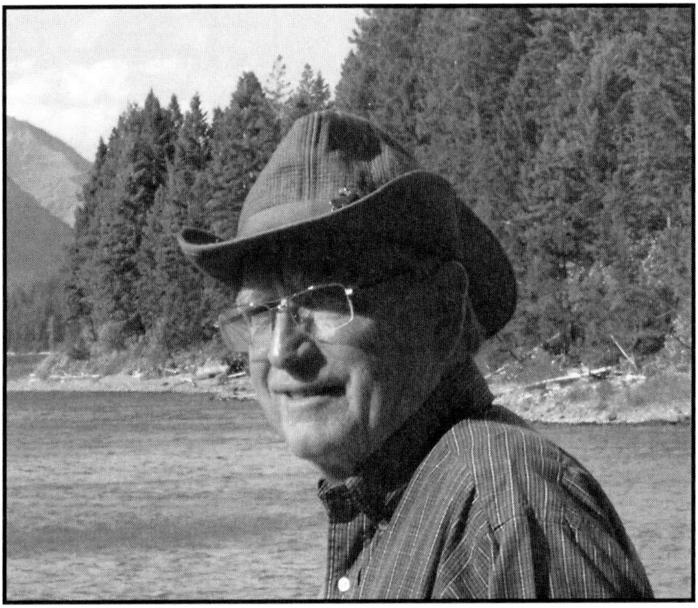

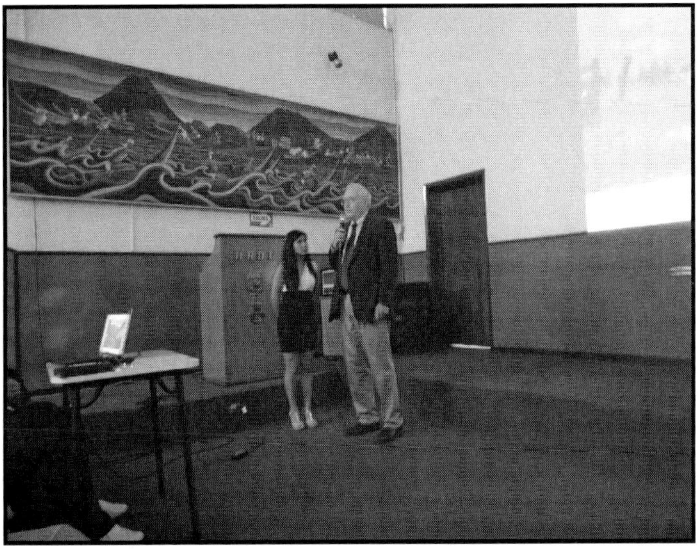